The Heart of Nalos

The Absurd Adventures: Volume 2

By Shawn Findlay

Read more absurd short stories on absurdscrolls.com

Table of Contents

Chapter 1: Into the Abyss

The sea was a deep shade of indigo, its surface glistening under the golden rays of the late afternoon sun. Seagulls circled overhead, their shrill cries occasionally piercing the tranquility of the coastal air. Jack Calloway, a young man with a fisherman's heart and wanderer's soul, sat alone in his small wooden boat. Today was like any other—calm, predictable. Or so he thought.

Jack had spent years fishing these waters, casting lines, reeling in the day's catch, and returning home to his humble seaside village. But there was always a nagging sense of something more lurking beneath the waves, something that called to him in his dreams. Today, his heart raced with a strange energy he couldn't explain, as if some force was guiding him to a different fate. The horizon seemed more distant, the air heavier with mystery.

The Catch of a Lifetime

Jack's line was cast far into the ocean's depths, disappearing into the void below. He leaned back, watching the clouds slowly drift across the sky. A gentle tug on the line interrupted his reverie, and instinctively, he grabbed the rod.

At first, the tug was subtle, but it quickly escalated into something fierce. The fishing rod bent at an unnatural angle, creaking under the strain. Jack braced himself, gripping the rod tightly. The force was far beyond anything he'd encountered. This was no ordinary fish.

Suddenly, his boat lurched violently, nearly knocking him overboard. His hands tightened around the rod, his knuckles white with tension. Whatever had taken his bait was dragging his boat at an alarming speed. The horizon blurred as the boat sliced through the water like a torpedo. Panic set in as the ocean shifted from its usual tranquil state to a rolling beast, waves crashing over the bow.

Jack struggled to regain control, but it was futile. The creature was too powerful, too determined. And then, without warning, the boat plunged downward, swallowed whole by the churning sea.

A Journey to the Other Side

Jack's breath caught in his throat as water engulfed him. The world turned into a swirl of dark blues and blacks, bubbles escaping from his lungs as he sank deeper. The pressure built around him, but the pull of the line continued, dragging him farther into the depths. His mind raced, struggling to comprehend what was happening. Was he drowning? Was this how it ended?

And then, just as suddenly as it began, the descent stopped.

Jack's eyes blinked open in astonishment. He was floating in an eerie calmness, suspended in water that shimmered with an ethereal glow. Tiny luminescent creatures swam past him, their colors rippling through the water like electric pulses.

Above him, there was no sign of the surface, only the strange shimmering light surrounding him.

Before he could take another breath—or question how he was breathing at all—an enormous shadow loomed from below. The shadow took shape, revealing itself to be a colossal fish, the likes of which Jack had never seen. Its scales shimmered in an array of colors, and its eyes were vast, ancient, and intelligent.

With a final flick of its tail, the fish propelled itself upward, taking Jack and his boat with it. The water churned again, but this time Jack didn't feel fear—only a strange sense of awe and inevitability.

The water around him began to ripple and twist, pulling reality apart as if the very fabric of the universe were unweaving. And then, in one final, disorienting burst, the creature spat him and his boat upward through the surface.

Jack gasped, blinking against the sudden brightness. His lungs burned with the intake of air, and as he wiped the saltwater from his eyes, he realized he was no longer in the world he knew.

The Mystical World of Nalos

Jack's boat bobbed on the surface of a new sea. The sky above was a vibrant violet, streaked with golden clouds that moved unnaturally fast. The water beneath him shimmered with a silvery hue, reflecting the odd-colored sky like a liquid mirror.

But what struck him most was the land that lay ahead—a massive island, unlike anything he'd ever seen. Its shoreline was made of sand that glittered like crushed diamonds, and towering trees with translucent leaves swayed in the distance. The air smelled sweet, like a mix of wildflowers and fresh rain.

Jack had no idea where he was, but something deep inside told him he had crossed into another world—a world of magic, mystery, and danger.

As he paddled closer to the island, Jack's heart raced with a mixture of fear and excitement. He had always dreamed of adventure, of something beyond the ordinary. And now, it seemed, he had found it.

The Enchanting Mermaid

The first signs of life Jack encountered were not on the shore but in the water beside him. A ripple disturbed the surface, and suddenly, a figure emerged—a woman, beautiful beyond imagination, her long hair flowing like liquid silver, her eyes shimmering like the stars. She was a mermaid—at least, when she was in the water. Her tail glistened in shades of teal and sapphire.

Jack stared, dumbfounded, as she swam closer. She smiled at him, a mischievous but kind smile, and spoke in a language that seemed to flow with the rhythm of the sea itself. Yet somehow, Jack understood her.

"I am Lyria," she said, her voice soft and melodic. "Welcome to Nalos."

Jack tried to respond but found himself tongue-tied, captivated by her beauty and the absurdity of his situation. Lyria swam circles around his boat, her movements graceful and hypnotic.

"You're not from here," she observed, tilting her head with curiosity. "I can sense it. You've been brought by the Deep One, haven't you?"

Jack nodded, still unable to form words.

Lyria's eyes softened with a mix of amusement and affection. "You'll need guidance here, Jack Calloway. This world is not like yours. It's filled with wonders... and dangers."

Jack's heart leaped at the sound of his name. How did she know? Was this all some elaborate dream?

Before he could ask, Lyria swam to the side of his boat and gracefully lifted herself halfway out of the water, her face mere inches from his.

"I'll protect you," she whispered, her voice filled with an undeniable promise. "We mermaids are bound to protect those we fall in love with."

Jack blinked in shock. "F-Fall in love?"

Lyria giggled, a sound that resonated like wind chimes in the air. "Yes. The moment I saw you, I knew. You'll come to understand soon enough."

Jack wasn't sure how to respond to this sudden declaration of love, especially from a mystical creature of the sea. But he couldn't deny the magnetic pull he felt toward her. Everything about Nalos was strange, enchanting, and somehow right.

The Island of Oddities

As Jack and Lyria reached the island, the strangeness only deepened. The moment Lyria's tail touched the shore, it transformed—fading into legs as her body shifted into that of a fully human woman. Her shimmering scales disappeared, replaced by smooth skin. She stood before Jack, now completely human, as if the sea and land each claimed different sides of her.

Jack blinked in astonishment as she smiled knowingly. "Here, on land, I am like you. But in the water, I return to my true form."

Together, they walked onto the glittering beach, where the sand sparkled with shifting patterns. The forest beyond was colorful. Gigantic flowers bloomed in radiant shades, and peculiar animals scurried about—creatures with wings where there should be none, or legs far too long for their tiny bodies.

In the distance, Jack could see massive structures, temples made of gemstone-like materials that glittered in the sun. Smoke rose from strange chimneys, but no houses or villages were visible. The whole island seemed to be alive, humming with energy.

As Jack and Lyria made their way inland, he began to notice something else—treasure. Scattered across the beach and tucked into the roots of trees were jewels, gold coins, and strange artifacts. Some were half-buried, while others gleamed openly under the sunlight.

"Is this... treasure?" Jack asked, astonished.

Lyria nodded, her expression unreadable. "It is. Nalos is full of such things. But be careful—treasure often comes with a price."

Jack knelt down and picked up a gleaming ruby the size of his fist. It was warm to the touch, pulsating with a strange energy. He could feel his mind drifting, drawn toward its power, but Lyria quickly snatched it from his hand.

"Not yet," she warned. "You're not ready."

Jack swallowed hard. This island—this world—was like nothing he had ever imagined. He had no idea how or why he had been brought here, but one thing was clear: his adventure was only beginning.

A New Reality

As the sun dipped lower in the violet sky, casting long shadows across the land, Jack stood at the edge of the strange forest. He turned to Lyria, now fully human, her eyes watching him with that same strange intensity.

"This world is beautiful," Jack said softly. "But... why me? Why am I here?"

Lyria smiled, her silver hair shimmering in the twilight. "The Deep One doesn't make mistakes. You were chosen, Jack. And soon, you'll discover why."

With that cryptic response, Lyria gazed out toward the sea, the waves crashing gently against the shore as her eyes sparkled with a mix of mystery and affection. Somewhere beyond the horizon lay answers Jack couldn't yet comprehend.

This was a place of magic, a place of wonder—and somewhere, deep within its heart, lay the answers to Jack's questions.

But first, he would need to survive the island of oddities.

Chapter 2: The Island of Secrets

The air on Nalos was intoxicating. Jack breathed it in, feeling
the weight of the world he had known melt away. The violet
sky overhead cast a warm, surreal glow, and the strange
island hummed with an energy that both excited and
unnerved him. Lyria, now fully human on land, walked
beside him, her bare feet leaving imprints on the shimmering
sand.

Jack's mind raced with a thousand questions. Why had the
Deep One brought him here? What dangers lurked beneath
the island's beauty? And, perhaps most pressing of all, why
had Lyria, this mysterious and enchanting creature, declared
her love for him so suddenly?

As they ventured deeper into the island, Jack couldn't shake
the feeling that the island itself was watching him. The trees
whispered in a language he couldn't quite understand, and
the ground beneath him seemed to pulse in time with his
heartbeat.

The Temple of Echoes

They reached a dense part of the forest where the trees
stood impossibly tall, their translucent leaves glowing with
an internal light. In the distance, the glittering temple Jack
had seen earlier came into view, towering above the forest
canopy like a beacon. The structure was breathtaking, made
of shimmering gemstone that changed color as the light
shifted, as if it were alive.

Lyria stopped, her eyes narrowing as they approached the temple's grand entrance. The large, arched doorway was carved with intricate symbols, some familiar, others entirely alien. She placed a hand on Jack's arm, stopping him.

"This is the Temple of Echoes," Lyria said softly, her voice echoing slightly off the surrounding trees. "It's one of the oldest places on Nalos, filled with knowledge and memories. But it's also filled with traps for the unwary."

Jack frowned. "Traps?"

She nodded. "Many come here seeking answers, treasures, or power. But the temple only gives what it chooses to give. And sometimes, it takes more than it returns."

Her warning hung in the air like a weight, but Jack felt a strange pull toward the temple. Something inside him— something deeper than curiosity—urged him forward. He had been brought here for a reason, after all. And maybe the answers he sought lay within.

"I need to see it," Jack said, his voice resolute. "I need to know why I'm here."

Lyria's gaze softened, and she nodded. "Very well. But stay close to me."

Together, they stepped through the arched entrance and into the heart of the temple.

Whispers of the Past

The interior of the Temple of Echoes was even more mesmerizing than Jack could have imagined. The walls were lined with enormous crystals that pulsed with a faint, rhythmic glow, casting a soft, ever-shifting light across the vast chamber. At first, the space seemed empty, but as Jack moved deeper into the room, the air around him thickened with energy, and faint whispers began to rise, as though the temple itself was speaking.

Jack strained to make out the words, but they remained just beyond his grasp, a chorus of indistinct murmurs that sent chills down his spine. The floor beneath them was smooth, reflecting the strange light from the crystals, and as they walked, Jack noticed images shifting on the surface—shadows of people, events, and places that seemed to flicker in and out of existence.

"These are the echoes," Lyria explained, her voice reverent. "This temple remembers everything. Every moment that has happened in Nalos is stored here, waiting to be found."

Jack stared down at the shifting images, mesmerized. Among the countless scenes, he saw flashes of great battles, ancient rituals, and faces that seemed vaguely familiar, though he couldn't place why.

And then, as if responding to his thoughts, the floor began to change. The shifting images slowed, coalescing into a single vision. Jack's breath caught in his throat as he recognized the figure standing in the center of the scene—it was him.

He watched as his own reflection stared back at him, standing on the same beach where he had first arrived. But something was different. His reflection held an object in his hand—a gleaming, golden orb that pulsed with a strange, otherworldly light.

"What is that?" Jack whispered, unable to tear his eyes away from the vision.

Lyria's expression darkened. "It's the Heart of Nalos. The source of the island's power."

Jack blinked. "The source of its power? Why would I be holding it?"

Lyria turned to face him fully, her eyes serious. "Because the Deep One chose you, Jack. You've been brought here to either protect the Heart... or destroy it."

An Unexpected Visitor

Before Jack could respond, the ground beneath them rumbled, sending a low vibration through the temple. The crystals lining the walls flickered, and the whispers grew louder, more urgent.

Lyria's eyes widened, and she grabbed Jack's arm. "We need to leave—now!"

But it was too late. A figure appeared at the far end of the chamber, stepping out of the shadows. He was tall, with a cloak made of shimmering black scales that glistened in the dim light. His face was concealed by a mask of bone, and his presence seemed to sap the air of warmth.

Jack's heart pounded in his chest as the figure approached. He moved with a grace that was almost inhuman, his steps soundless against the temple's floor.

"Who are you?" Jack demanded, his voice echoing in the vast chamber.

The figure stopped several paces away and tilted his head, regarding Jack with cold, unreadable eyes. When he spoke, his voice was low, but it carried a weight that seemed to press down on Jack's very soul.

"I am Kaldros," the figure said, his voice dripping with menace. "Guardian of the Heart."

Jack's mind raced. Kaldros? He had never heard the name before, but something about it sent a chill down his spine. The air around him seemed to thicken, and the whispers in the temple grew louder, almost frantic.

Lyria stepped forward, her posture tense. "Kaldros, the Heart belongs to Nalos. It's not for you to keep."

Kaldros chuckled, a sound that echoed unnervingly in the chamber. "Oh, Lyria. You've always been so naive. The Heart of Nalos is power incarnate. It belongs to whoever is strong enough to claim it."

Jack's grip tightened around the handle of his knife, though he knew it would be useless against someone—or something—like Kaldros.

"And you," Kaldros said, his gaze locking onto Jack. "The one chosen by the Deep One. You will have a choice soon enough: join me and take your rightful place as ruler of Nalos, or stand in my way and be destroyed."

Jack's blood ran cold. The words hung in the air like a challenge, daring him to decide his fate.

Before Jack could respond, the ground shook violently, and the walls of the temple groaned as cracks spread through the crystal. The whispers in the air grew to a deafening roar, and Jack instinctively reached for Lyria's hand.

"We have to get out of here!" Lyria shouted over the noise, pulling Jack toward the entrance.

Kaldros remained where he stood, his cold eyes watching them as they fled. "You cannot run from destiny," he called after them.

The Escape

Jack and Lyria raced out of the temple, the rumbling of the collapsing structure echoing behind them. As they broke through the trees and back into the open air, Jack gasped, his lungs burning from the sprint.

The violet sky above was now streaked with ominous clouds, and the once-calm sea was churning violently, as if reacting to the upheaval of the island's balance.

"What was that?" Jack asked breathlessly, glancing back at the temple, which now stood like a shattered ruin against the forest.

Lyria's face was pale, her expression grim. "That was Kaldros. He's been seeking the Heart for centuries. He's dangerous, Jack. More dangerous than you can imagine."

Jack nodded, still trying to process what had just happened. "And the Heart of Nalos? What is it really?"

Lyria's gaze met his, her eyes filled with a mixture of fear and determination. "The Heart is more than just a source of power, Jack. It's the very essence of this world. Whoever controls it controls Nalos. And Kaldros will stop at nothing to claim it for himself."

Jack swallowed hard. The weight of his situation was beginning to sink in. He hadn't just been brought to Nalos by chance—he had been chosen, drawn into a conflict that was far older and far more dangerous than he could have ever imagined.

But one thing was clear: Kaldros wouldn't stop until he had the Heart. And if Jack wanted to survive—if he wanted to protect this strange, beautiful world—he would have to find the Heart first.

Chapter 3: The Trials of Nalos

The island of Nalos hummed with life, more vibrant and surreal than ever before. As Jack and Lyria ventured away from the ruined Temple of Echoes, the urgency to find the Heart of Nalos weighed heavily on them. But the journey toward it wasn't a straight line. Nalos, with all its strangeness and unpredictability, had its own plans for the duo.

The sky, still painted with streaks of violet and gold, hinted at the mystery and magic embedded in every corner of this world. Though the Heart was their ultimate goal, Jack and Lyria were about to be drawn into a series of bizarre and dangerous adventures that would test their strength, their bond, and their resolve.

The Serpent of the Misty Marsh

Leaving the temple behind, Jack and Lyria made their way into the denser part of the island—a misty marsh that stretched as far as the eye could see. The air grew thick with moisture, the trees twisted and gnarled, their bark glowing faintly in the mist. Pools of murky water dotted the landscape, and strange creatures flitted through the shadows.

Jack couldn't shake the sense of unease that hung in the air. The whispers from the temple still echoed in his mind, and Kaldros's ominous words about the Heart of Nalos weighed heavily on him. As they trudged through the swampy terrain, Lyria remained unusually quiet.

"We need to keep moving," Jack said, breaking the silence. "The sooner we get through this marsh, the better."

Lyria nodded but said nothing. Her eyes scanned their surroundings warily, as if she sensed something lurking just beyond the mist.

It wasn't long before her instincts proved correct.

A low, guttural hiss filled the air, sending a chill down Jack's spine. He froze, his hand instinctively reaching for his knife, though he knew it would offer little protection against the dangers of Nalos.

From the depths of the marsh, a massive serpent emerged, its scales shimmering like oil slicks in the dim light. Its body coiled and twisted through the mist, and its eyes glowed an eerie green. The creature's head, large enough to swallow a man whole, hovered above them, its tongue flickering in and out like a whip.

"Stay still," Lyria whispered, her voice barely audible. "It's a Mist Serpent. It hunts by sensing movement."

Jack nodded, trying to keep his breathing steady as the serpent slithered closer. The creature's eyes locked onto them, unblinking and calculating. Jack could feel the tension in the air, a thin line between safety and destruction.

But just as the serpent seemed ready to strike, Lyria stepped forward, her hand raised in a calming gesture. She began to hum softly, a haunting melody that seemed to resonate with the very air around them. The serpent's body relaxed, its eyes losing their sharp focus. Slowly, it lowered its head, as if lulled into a trance.

"Come on," Lyria whispered to Jack, beckoning him to follow.

Carefully, they stepped around the serpent, moving as quietly as possible. Jack's heart raced, his muscles tense, but he trusted Lyria's lead. The Mist Serpent, still entranced by Lyria's song, remained motionless as they slipped away.

Once they were a safe distance away, Jack let out a breath he hadn't realized he was holding. "That was incredible," he said, his voice still hushed from the tension.

Lyria smiled faintly. "The creatures of Nalos are bound to its magic. They can be dangerous, but they can also be swayed."

Jack nodded, marveling at Lyria's connection to this mystical world. As they continued through the marsh, the mist began to thin, revealing more of the strange, dreamlike landscape.

But the encounter with the Mist Serpent had been a reminder: this world was beautiful, yes—but it was also perilous.

The Village of Shadows

By the time they emerged from the marsh, the sky had deepened into twilight. The strange trees that lined the path ahead cast long shadows across the ground, their branches twisting and curling like dark tendrils. In the distance, Jack spotted the flicker of firelight—a village, nestled among the trees.

"That's the Village of Shadows," Lyria said, her voice tinged with caution. "It's a place of refuge for some, but it's also... complicated."

"Complicated how?" Jack asked.

Lyria hesitated. "The villagers here live between worlds. They're neither fully part of Nalos nor fully outside it. They've been touched by the island's magic in ways that are... unsettling."

Despite her warning, they had little choice but to continue toward the village. The last rays of sunlight were fading, and spending the night out in the open wilderness of Nalos was not an option.

As they entered the village, Jack noticed the peculiar nature of its inhabitants. The people moved like shadows, their forms flickering as if caught between realities. Their eyes glowed faintly, and their voices echoed as if coming from a great distance.

One of the villagers, a tall man with silver hair and hollow eyes, stepped forward to greet them.

"Travelers," he said, his voice carrying a strange, distorted resonance. "Welcome to the Village of Shadows. You may rest here, but be mindful of the night."

Lyria bowed her head slightly in respect. "Thank you, Eldrin. We seek shelter for the night and safe passage through your lands."

Eldrin's gaze lingered on Jack, his hollow eyes studying him with unsettling intensity. "You carry a heavy burden," Eldrin said, his voice almost a whisper. "The Heart calls to you."

Jack stiffened. "How do you know about the Heart?"

Eldrin smiled faintly, though the gesture didn't reach his eyes. "This village exists in the spaces between Nalos and its many realities. We know much of what happens in this world, and the Heart is the key to it all."

Jack exchanged a glance with Lyria, who seemed equally unsettled by Eldrin's words.

"Rest," Eldrin said, gesturing toward a small hut near the center of the village. "But be cautious. The night in Nalos has its own magic, and it's not always kind."

The Night of Visions

Inside the small, dimly lit hut, Jack and Lyria sat in silence. The flickering light from the village fires cast eerie shadows on the walls, and the faint echoes of the villagers' voices drifted through the air like a haunting melody.

Jack couldn't shake the feeling that the village was watching them, even when the villagers weren't present. There was a palpable tension in the air, a sense that the boundaries between worlds were thinner here.

"I don't trust them," Jack admitted, keeping his voice low.

Lyria nodded in agreement. "The Village of Shadows is a strange place, even for Nalos. But for now, we don't have many options."

Jack lay down on the straw bed, staring up at the thatched roof as his thoughts swirled. The weight of the Heart of Nalos pressed on his mind. Why had he been chosen? And what was he supposed to do with it? Kaldros's offer still echoed in his head—join him, or be destroyed. But Jack knew he couldn't trust Kaldros. There was something deeply wrong with the man, something dark and corrupt.

As Jack's thoughts drifted, exhaustion began to overtake him. He closed his eyes, letting the quiet hum of the village lull him to sleep.

But sleep in the Village of Shadows was not like sleep in the world Jack had known.

Jack awoke to a different world. The hut was gone, and instead, he stood in an open field under a sky filled with swirling colors—vivid reds, deep purples, and shimmering golds. The ground beneath him was soft, like a living thing, and the air buzzed with energy.

In the distance, a figure approached—tall, cloaked in black, with eyes like burning coals.

"Kaldros," Jack whispered, his heart racing.

The dark figure smiled, though it was a cold, cruel smile. "You cannot run from your destiny, Jack Calloway."

Jack reached for his knife, but it wasn't there. He was unarmed, defenseless.

Kaldros took a step closer, his voice low and menacing. "The Heart will be mine, one way or another. You can fight it, but you cannot win."

The ground beneath Jack began to tremble, and the swirling sky grew darker, the colors fading into blackness. Jack tried to move, but his feet were rooted to the spot, trapped by some unseen force.

Kaldros's voice echoed in his mind. "Choose wisely, Jack. For when the time comes, there will be no turning back."

With a start, Jack awoke. The hut was still around him, the dim light from the village fires flickering through the cracks in the walls. His heart pounded in his chest, and his skin was damp with sweat.

Lyria was beside him, her expression concerned. "You had a vision, didn't you?"

Jack nodded, swallowing hard. "Kaldros. He was there... he said the Heart would be his."

Lyria's face darkened. "The Village of Shadows has a way of drawing out visions from the mind. It's part of their nature. But it's also a warning, Jack. Kaldros is not going to stop."

Jack sat up, running a hand through his hair. "I know. We need to find the Heart before he does. But every step we take... it feels like we're getting further from it."

Lyria placed a hand on his shoulder. "We'll find it, Jack. But Nalos has its own path for us to follow. There's more we need to learn, more we need to face, before we can confront the Heart."

Jack met her gaze, feeling a sense of calm despite the chaos swirling around them. He didn't know what lay ahead, but he knew one thing for certain: he wasn't facing it alone.

And that, at least, gave him hope.

Chapter 4: The Bonds of Destiny

The sun rose over Nalos, casting a warm golden light across the landscape. Jack and Lyria stepped out of the hut in the Village of Shadows, their minds still buzzing from the surreal experiences of the previous night. Though they had shared a moment of intimacy in the darkness, the weight of their quest pressed heavily on both of them.

As they looked out over the village, Jack felt a surge of determination. He turned to Lyria, her silhouette framed by the dawn's light, and his heart raced. It was becoming harder to ignore the deepening connection between them—a bond forged not only in danger but also in mutual understanding and affection.

A Journey Through the Glimmering Grove

"We should continue our search for the Heart," Jack said, trying to keep his voice steady. "But I want to know more about this place and the people in it."

Lyria smiled, her eyes sparkling with warmth. "I know of a place called the Glimmering Grove. It's a forest filled with magical flora and curious beings. If anyone knows about the Heart, it might be the creatures of the Grove."

"Let's go then," Jack replied, his spirit buoyed by her enthusiasm.

They made their way through the Village of Shadows, leaving behind the flickering lights and whispers. The village was awakening, its inhabitants moving like shadows, and Jack couldn't help but feel a pang of gratitude for their hospitality, despite the unease that hung in the air.

As they ventured deeper into the heart of the island, the terrain shifted. Trees with luminescent leaves stretched toward the sky, casting a variety of colors across the ground. The path was lined with flowers that pulsed with an ethereal glow, and the air was filled with a sweet, intoxicating scent that stirred something deep within Jack.

"This place is breathtaking," Jack said, his voice filled with awe. He turned to Lyria, who was watching him with a soft smile. "You've been here before?"

"Many times," she replied, her expression thoughtful. "The Glimmering Grove is a sanctuary. It's where magic is alive, and the spirits of the island dwell. They can be mischievous, but they're also wise."

Jack felt a flutter in his chest at her words. There was something about Lyria's presence that made the world around him feel more vibrant, more alive. He wanted to know everything about her, about the island, and about the bond they were forging amidst the chaos.

The Guardian of the Grove

As they ventured deeper into the Glimmering Grove, a low hum began to resonate through the air. The sound grew louder, enveloping them in a warm embrace, and Jack felt a strange energy coursing through him.

Suddenly, the ground trembled beneath their feet, and from the shadows emerged a figure. A tall being made entirely of vines and flowers stepped into view, its face a blend of natural beauty and fierce determination. Its eyes glowed with an emerald light, and a crown of flowers adorned its head.

"Welcome, travelers," the being said, its voice a melodic whisper. "I am Thalia, Guardian of the Glimmering Grove. What brings you to my realm?"

Jack stepped forward, captivated by Thalia's presence. "We seek the Heart of Nalos," he declared, his voice steady. "We believe that the creatures of this grove might know its whereabouts."

Thalia regarded them thoughtfully, the light in its eyes flickering. "The Heart is a powerful entity, tied to the essence of Nalos itself. Many seek it, but few understand its significance. Why do you pursue it?"

"We need to protect it from Kaldros," Lyria interjected, her voice firm. "He intends to use it for his own dark purposes. We cannot let that happen."

Thalia's expression softened, and the vines that formed its body rustled gently. "Kaldros has long sought the Heart, driven by ambition and greed. But there are trials you must face if you wish to find it. The Heart cannot be claimed easily."

Jack felt a thrill of excitement mixed with apprehension. "What kind of trials?"

"The Grove is alive with magic," Thalia explained. "It will test your bond and your resolve. Only through understanding and unity can you navigate its depths and uncover the Heart's secrets."

Lyria turned to Jack, her eyes searching his. "Are you ready for this?"

"I'm ready," Jack replied, his voice steady. "With you by my side, I can face anything."

The Trials of the Heart

Thalia led them deeper into the Grove, where the air shimmered with magic, and the landscape shifted and changed like a living tapestry. As they walked, Jack felt an unexplainable energy between him and Lyria, an invisible thread binding their fates together.

They reached a clearing where a circle of ancient stones stood, each inscribed with runes that glowed softly. "This is where the trials will begin," Thalia announced. "You must face three challenges—each one designed to test your hearts and your unity."

Jack's heart raced at the thought. He took Lyria's hand, intertwining their fingers. "We can do this together," he said, his eyes locked onto hers.

Thalia nodded, stepping back. "The first trial will test your courage."

As the words left Thalia's lips, the air around them shifted, and a swirling mist enveloped the clearing. Jack could feel his heart pounding in his chest as shadows danced within the fog, forming into dark figures that loomed ominously.

"Face your fears," Thalia instructed. "Only by confronting what haunts you can you hope to move forward."

Jack felt the shadows closing in around them, dark whispers echoing in his mind. Images of his past—his failures, his loneliness—began to surface, each one a reminder of the doubts he carried. He struggled against the shadows, feeling their weight pressing down on him.

But then he looked at Lyria. Her presence grounded him, a beacon of light in the darkness. He squeezed her hand tightly, drawing strength from her warmth. "I won't let you go," he said, his voice steady.

With renewed determination, Jack stepped forward, confronting the shadows. "You don't own me," he declared. "I'm not afraid of you anymore!"

The shadows recoiled, fading into the mist as Jack's courage broke their hold. Lyria's eyes shone with pride, and Jack felt a surge of triumph.

"Well done," Thalia said, emerging from the mist. "You've faced your fears and emerged stronger. But there are more challenges ahead."

The Bond of Trust

The mist cleared, revealing a new setting. They stood in a serene glade, a crystal-clear pool of water shimmering in the center. The air was filled with the sound of gentle laughter, echoing like music.

"This is the second trial," Thalia explained. "You must demonstrate your trust in one another. Only by surrendering to each other can you progress."

Jack exchanged a glance with Lyria, confusion flickering in her eyes. "What do we need to do?"

"Trust can take many forms," Thalia replied. "You must each enter the water and allow the Grove to reveal your true selves. The experience may be disorienting, but you must trust each other to navigate it."

With a deep breath, Jack stepped forward, the cool water lapping against his feet. He glanced back at Lyria, who nodded, her expression resolute. They both waded into the pool, the water enveloping them in a gentle embrace.

As they submerged, the world around them shifted. Jack felt weightless, as if he were floating in a dream. Colors swirled around him, images of moments from his life flashing by— moments of joy, heartbreak, and connection.

Suddenly, he found himself standing on a shore, a different version of himself facing a reflection in the water. In that reflection, he saw Lyria, but she was shimmering, her true mermaid form emerging beneath the surface. Her laughter echoed in the air, filling him with warmth.

Jack reached out, but the water rippled and distorted her image. "Lyria!" he called, desperation creeping into his voice.

Then he heard her voice, strong and clear. "Trust, Jack! Trust that I will always find you!"

In that moment, he felt the bond between them solidify. He stepped closer, focusing on her essence—their shared adventures, their laughter, and their burgeoning love. With every ounce of faith, he plunged into the water, feeling the coolness envelop him.

When he emerged, he was back in the glade, Lyria beside him, her eyes bright with understanding.

"Well done," Thalia said, her voice echoing with approval. "You've passed the second trial, demonstrating your trust in one another."

Jack smiled, feeling a rush of exhilaration. "We did it!"

The Final Challenge

With two trials completed, Jack and Lyria felt an undeniable sense of accomplishment. But the air was thick with anticipation as Thalia prepared them for the final challenge.

"The last trial will test your love for one another," Thalia explained. "In the depths of the Grove, you will face an illusion—a choice that will challenge your very hearts. Only through unwavering love can you overcome it."

As Thalia led them deeper into the grove, the surroundings shifted once more, transforming into a dark forest where shadows danced menacingly. The atmosphere was heavy, charged with an energy that made Jack's skin prickle.

They reached a clearing illuminated by a soft, golden light. At its center stood a beautiful tree, its branches heavy with glowing fruits, each pulsing with a heartbeat of its own.

"Choose wisely," Thalia warned. "Each fruit offers a different path, but only one will lead you to the Heart of Nalos."

Jack stepped forward, entranced by the sight. "Lyria, we have to choose together," he said, feeling the weight of the decision pressing on him.

Lyria's brow furrowed as she studied the tree. "But what if we choose wrong? What if it leads us away from the Heart?"

"Then we'll face it together," Jack replied, determination in his voice. "Whatever happens, I trust you."

With their hands clasped tightly, they examined the fruits. Each one whispered promises—adventure, power, love, and knowledge. The allure was intoxicating, but Jack felt a sense of clarity in Lyria's presence.

"Let's choose the fruit that resonates with our hearts," Lyria said, her voice steady. "Not what we think we need, but what we truly desire."

Jack nodded, and they moved closer to the tree, each fruit glowing with its own light. Together, they reached for the fruit that pulsed gently, emitting a warm glow that enveloped them in comfort.

As they plucked the fruit from the branch, the ground trembled beneath them, and a brilliant light enveloped the clearing. They were swept into a whirlwind of colors and sensations, their surroundings shifting in a kaleidoscope of magic.

When the light subsided, they found themselves standing in a vast expanse, the Heart of Nalos floating before them—a brilliant jewel pulsing with life and energy.

The Heart of Nalos

"Jack!" Lyria exclaimed, her eyes wide with wonder.

Jack felt an overwhelming sense of awe as he reached for the Heart. But just as his fingers brushed against it, a dark shadow loomed over them. Kaldros emerged from the darkness, a cruel smile on his lips.

"Fools," he sneered. "You think you can take the Heart? It belongs to me!"

"Stay back, Kaldros!" Jack shouted, his heart racing. He felt Lyria's presence beside him, a grounding force amidst the chaos.

Kaldros laughed, his voice echoing with malice. "You are too late. The Heart will bring me the power I crave, and you will be nothing but a memory."

But Jack stood firm, drawing strength from Lyria. "We won't let you take it! We have come too far, and our love is stronger than your darkness."

Kaldros's laughter turned to rage, and he lunged forward. But Jack and Lyria stood resolute, their hands intertwined, channeling their bond into a shield of light.

The brilliance of their love clashed with Kaldros's darkness, illuminating the void around them. The Heart pulsed in response, resonating with their united energy, and the world shook with the force of their connection.

The Power of Love

In that moment, Jack realized that their love was not just a feeling; it was a force that transcended time and space. They were not just fighting for the Heart of Nalos; they were fighting for their right to exist in this world and the bond they had forged.

"Together!" Lyria shouted, her voice filled with determination.

They pressed forward, their combined energy surging toward Kaldros, pushing back the darkness that enveloped him. The air crackled with magic, and in an explosive burst of light, Kaldros was engulfed in the radiance of their love.

When the light faded, Kaldros was gone, his darkness dissipated into nothingness. Jack and Lyria stood together, breathing heavily as they gazed at the Heart of Nalos, still floating before them.

"Did we do it?" Jack whispered, awe-struck.

Lyria smiled, her eyes shimmering with tears of joy. "I think we did."

With a final surge of energy, the Heart descended into their hands, radiating warmth and life. They felt the connection to Nalos deepen, a pulse that resonated with their very souls.

A New Beginning

As the energy of the Heart flowed through them, Jack and Lyria exchanged a glance filled with unspoken promises. They had faced their fears, their trust had been tested, and their love had triumphed over darkness. This was not just the beginning of their journey; it was the foundation of a bond that would shape their destiny.

"Where do we go from here?" Jack asked, the Heart still glowing brightly in their hands.

Lyria looked up at him, a spark of determination in her eyes. "We protect it. We ensure that Kaldros never returns to claim it. Together, we can safeguard the Heart of Nalos."

Jack nodded, feeling a swell of pride and love for her. "Together."

As they turned to leave the clearing, the world around them shimmered with newfound energy, the colors of Nalos brightening in response to the Heart's presence. They had faced the trials of the Grove, and they had emerged stronger, united by their shared journey and the love they had discovered.

And as they stepped into the embrace of the Glimmering Grove, Jack knew that whatever challenges lay ahead, they would face them side by side.

Chapter 5: The Heart's Disappearance

The warm glow of dawn filtered through the trees of the Glimmering Grove, painting the world in hues of gold and green. Jack and Lyria stirred in their makeshift bed, nestled among the vibrant foliage. The Heart of Nalos pulsed softly between them, a constant reminder of their victory over Kaldros.

But as the morning light illuminated their surroundings, Jack felt an unsettling sense of emptiness. He blinked and stretched, glancing at Lyria, whose serene expression mirrored the tranquility of the grove. They had battled darkness and emerged victorious, but a gnawing sense of dread hung in the air.

A Night of Lost Dreams

As they prepared to rise, Jack reached for the Heart, only to find the space where it had rested empty. Panic surged within him. "Lyria! The Heart!"

Lyria's eyes shot open, confusion quickly giving way to alarm. "What do you mean? It was right here!"

Jack bolted upright, scanning their surroundings. The grove looked unchanged, but the absence of the Heart cast a shadow over the beauty. "It was here when we fell asleep. Where could it have gone?"

Lyria sprang to her feet, urgency sparking in her gaze. "We need to find it! If Kaldros discovers it's missing…"

A cold shiver ran down Jack's spine at the thought. Kaldros had been defeated, but he had not been eradicated. The dark sorcerer would do anything to regain control of the Heart, and they had to act fast.

Into the Unknown

They rushed back toward the Village of Shadows, their minds racing. Thalia would know what to do; she had guided them through the trials and had a connection to the Grove's magic. As they entered the village, its inhabitants moved about, oblivious to their impending danger.

"Thalia!" Lyria called out, her voice cutting through the morning air.

The Guardian emerged from the shadows, her expression grave. "You look troubled, young ones. What has transpired?"

"The Heart is gone," Jack explained, the urgency in his voice evident. "We woke up, and it was missing. We fear Kaldros might find it again."

Thalia's expression darkened. "The Heart of Nalos is a beacon of power. It can draw others to it, especially those who covet its strength. We must act quickly."

Jack felt a weight settle in his chest. "What do we do?"

"You must search the Grove and beyond. It could be hidden in a place only accessible to those who are worthy," Thalia advised. "Follow the whispers of the wind; they will guide you to where the Heart may be."

With newfound determination, Jack and Lyria set out once more into the mystical landscape, their hearts pounding with urgency.

Following the Whispers

As they traversed the vibrant grove, Jack strained to listen to the faint whispers carried by the wind. "What do you hear?" Lyria asked, her gaze fixed on him.

"I can't make it out yet," Jack replied, focusing intently. "It's like a melody, a call beckoning us."

"Maybe it's leading us to a clue about the Heart's location," Lyria suggested.

But as they ventured deeper into the grove, the whispers grew fainter, replaced by an eerie silence. Jack's heart sank as he realized the absence of guidance left them lost in uncertainty.

"Where do we go from here?" Lyria asked, her brow furrowed in concern.

Jack sighed, frustration creeping in. "I don't know. I wish I could make sense of it all."

Lyria took his hand, squeezing it gently. "We'll figure it out together. But first, tell me about your past. I want to know more about you, Jack."

A Tale of Loss and Resilience

Jack hesitated for a moment, memories flooding back—the chaos, the pain, and the loneliness that had defined his early years. "I grew up in a small coastal town," he began, his voice quiet. "My parents died in a terrible accident when I was just a boy. A wreck. A storm hit while they were driving home. I was left all alone."

Lyria's expression softened, her eyes filled with empathy. "I'm so sorry, Jack."

He continued, his heart heavy with the weight of his words. "An old fisherman named Charlie took me in. He was a friend of my parents and raised me like I was his own. He taught me how to fish, how to survive. But he died too, from a grave illness, leaving me alone once more."

Lyria listened intently, her heart aching for him. "That must have been so hard for you."

Jack nodded, swallowing the lump in his throat. "I didn't have much reason to return to my old life after that. I had lost everything. But now..." His voice trailed off as he looked at Lyria. "Now, I'm discovering a new purpose. I've found something worth fighting for."

A New Purpose

Lyria smiled, her eyes sparkling with understanding. "You've found love, Jack. You've found a new family here in Nalos."

Jack felt warmth spread through him at her words. "I never thought I'd have a chance to experience this kind of connection again. It's terrifying, but it's also beautiful."

Suddenly, a rustling in the bushes interrupted their moment. Jack tensed, instinctively reaching for the dagger at his waist. Out of the foliage emerged a small creature—a shimmering sprite, with translucent wings that glowed in the sunlight.

"Help! Help!" the sprite squeaked, its tiny voice high-pitched and frantic.

"What's wrong?" Lyria asked, crouching down to the sprite's level.

"The shadows! They're coming!" the sprite exclaimed, trembling. "They've taken something important from the Heart!"

"Shadows?" Jack repeated, glancing at Lyria. "Are they Kaldros's minions?"

The sprite nodded vigorously. "They're stealing the Heart's magic, spreading darkness across the Grove! You must stop them!"

A Race Against Time

Jack's heart raced. This was not just about retrieving the Heart anymore; it was about protecting the entire realm from Kaldros's darkness. "Where do we find them?" he asked the sprite.

"Follow me! They're in the Forgotten Hollow!" the sprite shouted, darting off into the woods.

Jack and Lyria exchanged a determined glance before following the sprite. They raced through the grove, dodging branches and weaving between the colorful flora. Jack's heart pounded in his chest, fueled by the urgency of their mission.

As they approached the Forgotten Hollow, a foreboding darkness loomed ahead. The atmosphere shifted, and Jack felt a chill in the air, as if the very essence of the grove had been tainted.

The sprite led them to the edge of the Hollow, where shadows twisted and coiled around gnarled trees. "They're hiding in there!" it exclaimed.

"We need to be careful," Lyria said, her voice low. "We don't know what we're up against."

"Whatever it is, we face it together," Jack reassured her. He could feel the weight of their mission pressing down on them, but he also felt the strength of their bond. They had faced darkness before; they could do it again.

The Forgotten Hollow

Stepping into the Forgotten Hollow, the light dimmed, and the shadows deepened. The air grew thick with tension, and Jack gripped Lyria's hand tightly as they ventured further in. The whispers of the grove faded, replaced by an unsettling silence.

Suddenly, shadowy figures emerged from the darkness, their forms twisting and writhing like smoke. Jack's heart raced as he prepared to confront them.

"Stay close!" he urged, pulling Lyria beside him.

The shadow creatures lunged, their forms shifting and morphing as they advanced. Jack brandished his dagger, its blade glinting in the faint light. He swung at the nearest creature, but it dissolved into a puff of darkness, reforming behind him.

"Jack, watch out!" Lyria shouted, her voice piercing through the chaos.

He turned just in time to dodge another shadow, but it grazed his arm, sending a jolt of cold energy through him. He gritted his teeth, pushing through the pain. "We need to find the source of their power!"

Lyria nodded, her eyes focused. "Let's move!"

A Desperate Search

They fought their way through the shadows, Jack and Lyria working in tandem. He struck at the creatures, while Lyria summoned her own magic, channeling the energy of the grove to push the shadows back. But with each passing moment, Jack felt their strength wane, the shadows relentless in their pursuit.

"Where are they coming from?" he shouted, glancing at Lyria.

"I don't know! But we can't let them overwhelm us!" she replied, determination fueling her words.

In the heart of the hollow, they spotted a glowing orb pulsating with dark energy. It hovered above a twisted altar, surrounded by the shadow creatures. "That must be it!" Lyria exclaimed, pointing toward the orb.

Jack nodded, his heart racing. "If we can destroy it, we might be able to weaken the shadows!"

"Let's do it!" Lyria shouted, rushing forward.

With every ounce of strength they had left, they charged toward the altar. Jack slashed through the shadows, creating a path for Lyria. She raised her hands, drawing on the power of the grove, and a bright light erupted from her fingertips.

The light clashed with the darkness, illuminating the hollow. Jack felt hope surge within him, but the shadows pushed back, threatening to engulf them.

Facing the Darkness

"Together, Lyria!" Jack shouted, his voice steady amidst the chaos. "We can do this!"

With a fierce determination, they focused their energy on the orb, channeling their love and the magic of Nalos. The orb crackled with power, and the shadows writhed in agony as the light enveloped them.

"Now!" Lyria shouted, and they unleashed their combined magic at the orb. The explosion of light shattered the darkness, sending shockwaves through the hollow.

The shadows dissipated, retreating into the corners of the grove, and the orb shattered, releasing a wave of energy that washed over them. Jack felt warmth and clarity flood through him as the grove around them brightened.

"We did it!" Lyria exclaimed, her eyes shining.

Jack turned to her, elation surging through him. "We did!"

But their celebration was short-lived as they heard a familiar, sinister laughter echoing through the hollow. "You think you can escape me that easily?" Kaldros's voice boomed, sending chills down their spines.

The Rising Threat

From the depths of the darkness, Kaldros emerged, his presence heavy and malevolent. "You may have temporarily weakened my shadows, but I will always return. The Heart of Nalos will be mine!"

Jack's heart raced. They had only delayed the inevitable. "We'll never let you take it!" he shouted, stepping protectively in front of Lyria.

Kaldros sneered, his eyes narrowing. "Foolish boy. Your love will be your downfall."

"Don't listen to him, Jack!" Lyria urged, her voice steady despite the tension.

But as Kaldros unleashed a surge of dark energy, Jack felt the pull of despair creep into his heart. The shadows twisted around him, and he struggled to maintain his resolve.

An Unbreakable Bond

In that moment, Lyria grasped Jack's hand, her warmth igniting a spark within him. "We're stronger together!" she declared, her voice cutting through the darkness.

Jack looked at her, his heart swelling with determination. "You're right. Together."

Channeling their combined strength, they stood firm against Kaldros's onslaught. The light from their bond illuminated the hollow, pushing back the encroaching shadows.

As they faced Kaldros, Jack realized that they had something the dark sorcerer could never understand—an unbreakable bond forged in love and resilience. "You may have power, Kaldros, but you will never have what we share."

With a roar of defiance, they unleashed their energy once more, the brilliance overwhelming the darkness. Kaldros staggered back, fury etched on his face. "You will pay for this!"

A New Adventure Begins

With a final surge, Kaldros vanished into the shadows, leaving the hollow quiet once more. Jack and Lyria stood together, breathing heavily as the grove began to heal around them.

"We did it," Jack whispered, disbelief washing over him.

"But we still need to find the Heart," Lyria reminded him, her eyes filled with determination. "Kaldros won't give up. We have to protect it."

Jack nodded, feeling the weight of their mission. They may have won a battle, but the war was far from over. "Where do we go next?"

Lyria paused, considering. "The whispers we heard earlier... maybe they were leading us to another clue."

"Let's follow them," Jack suggested, feeling the stirrings of hope once more.

As they stepped out of the Forgotten Hollow, a sense of renewed purpose filled their hearts. They had faced darkness and emerged stronger, and now they would continue their quest to protect the Heart of Nalos and discover the secrets of this mystical world.

And as they ventured forward, Jack felt an unshakeable bond forming between them, a love that would carry them through the trials yet to come.

Chapter 6: Captured in the Depths

The Glimmering Grove had begun to regain its radiance after the battle with Kaldros, but the quest for the Heart of Nalos wasn't over. Jack and Lyria walked side by side, their connection deepening with each step, their mission still clear in their minds. The Heart, lost during the night, had left an empty void in their victory. Now, as they followed the faint whispers of magic through the forest, Jack couldn't shake the feeling that something—something sinister—was watching them.

Lyria's eyes scanned the surroundings, her brows knit in concentration. "Jack, do you hear that?"

Jack stopped in his tracks, listening. The forest had fallen eerily silent. No whispers, no wind, no signs of life. His pulse quickened. "We're not alone."

Before they could react, a sudden gust of wind swirled around them, and shadows lunged from the trees. Dark figures shrouded in cloaks appeared, surrounding them with no warning.

"Run, Lyria!" Jack shouted, grabbing her hand, but it was too late.

With a blur of motion, the figures seized them, dragging them into the depths of the forest. The world spun as they were enveloped in darkness.

The Prison of Shadows

When Jack opened his eyes, a cold, damp air filled his lungs. He sat up, his wrists bound by rough rope, and looked around. They were in a dimly lit cave, illuminated only by flickering torches along the walls. The air smelled of sea salt and decay, and the sound of distant water echoed off the stone walls.

Lyria lay nearby, unconscious but breathing steadily. Jack's heart sank as he realized the severity of their situation. They had been captured, but by whom? And why?

"Lyria," Jack whispered, gently shaking her. She stirred, blinking up at him.

"Where are we?" she asked, her voice groggy.

"I don't know," Jack replied, glancing around. "But we're not alone."

As if on cue, the shadows at the far end of the cave parted, revealing a tall figure dressed in dark robes, their face hidden behind a mask. Several more cloaked figures stood behind him, watching with eerie silence.

"Welcome, travelers," the masked figure said in a deep, cold voice. "We have been expecting you."

Jack's pulse raced. "Who are you? What do you want with us?"

The figure stepped closer, the flickering torchlight casting ominous shadows across his form. "I am the Keeper of the Depths, and we require your assistance."

Lyria, now fully alert, stood beside Jack. "Assistance? With what?"

The Keeper's gaze, though hidden behind the mask, seemed to pierce through them. "We have a task for you. A mission that only you can complete. You have the skills we need."

Jack frowned, confused. "We're not here to help you. We're searching for something important—"

The Keeper cut him off. "The Heart of Nalos, yes. We know of your quest, but your search is not of interest to us. Our need for you lies elsewhere."

Lyria narrowed her eyes, her voice defiant. "We're not here to do your bidding. Let us go."

The Keeper let out a slow, deliberate chuckle. "You will help us, or you will never leave this place."

An Underwater World

The Keeper motioned to his followers, and two of them stepped forward, dragging a heavy stone map from the shadows. It was etched with intricate patterns and runes, its surface glowing faintly with blue light. The map depicted a vast underwater kingdom, shimmering with mysterious beauty and danger.

"This is the Abyssal Realm," the Keeper explained. "A world beneath the oceans of Nalos, where ancient magic still lingers. There is an object deep within its waters that we need, an artifact lost to time. Only one who can traverse both land and sea can retrieve it."

Lyria's eyes widened. "You mean me. You need me because I can transform into a mermaid."

The Keeper nodded. "Indeed. And you," he said, turning to Jack, "will accompany her. For only those bound by trust and love can unlock the gates to the Abyssal Realm."

Jack felt a chill run down his spine. "And if we refuse?"

The Keeper's voice dropped to a menacing whisper. "Then you will rot in this cave, forever cut off from the outside world, and from your quest to find the Heart."

Lyria glanced at Jack, her face etched with worry. "We can't be trapped here forever," she whispered.

Jack clenched his fists, his mind racing. "We need to find a way out. We can't trust them."

Devising a Plan

Once the cloaked figures had left them alone, Jack and Lyria sat against the cold stone wall, their minds churning with possible plans for escape. The weight of their capture bore down on them, but neither was willing to give in to despair.

"Do you think we can escape on our own?" Lyria asked, her voice quiet but determined.

Jack glanced around the cave, searching for any potential weak points. The entrance was heavily guarded, and the walls were too smooth to climb. Their only chance was to outsmart their captors. "We have to, but it won't be easy."

Lyria frowned, her eyes filled with concern. "What if… what if we pretended to go along with their plan? We could buy ourselves some time and look for a way out while we're underwater."

Jack considered it. "It's risky. But if we refuse, they might never let us go."

Lyria nodded. "If we play along, we might be able to find the artifact they're after and use it to our advantage."

Jack looked at her, admiration in his eyes. "You're brilliant, you know that?"

She smiled, but the tension in the air remained. "We're in this together, Jack. We always have been."

Their plan was tentative, but it was the best option they had. They would pretend to comply with the Keeper's demands and use the underwater mission as a chance to escape. But there were still so many unknowns—what was this Abyssal Realm? And what dangers lurked within it?

The Keeper's Mission

The next day, the Keeper returned, his presence as cold and commanding as before. Jack and Lyria stood side by side, determined but cautious.

"We've made our decision," Jack said firmly. "We'll help you."

The Keeper inclined his head. "Wise. You will be taken to the entrance of the Abyssal Realm tomorrow. Prepare yourselves, for the journey is perilous, and few who enter the realm ever return."

Lyria stepped forward, her voice steady. "What exactly are we retrieving for you?"

The Keeper's gaze shifted to the stone map. "The Abyssal Key. It is an ancient artifact capable of unlocking the gates to the Lost City beneath the ocean. It has been hidden for centuries, guarded by the Leviathan—a creature of immense power. You will need both courage and skill to succeed."

Jack exchanged a glance with Lyria. "And once we retrieve this key, you'll let us go?"

The Keeper's voice turned ominous. "If you survive, yes."

The Keeper's followers appeared, leading them back to their dim cell to rest before the mission. As the heavy stone door closed behind them, Jack sat down beside Lyria, his mind racing.

"Do you think we can trust them to let us go once we have the key?" Lyria asked, doubt creeping into her voice.

"No," Jack said bluntly. "I don't think we can. That's why we need to find a way to escape as soon as we're out of this cave."

Lyria sighed, leaning her head on his shoulder. "It feels like we're constantly being pulled into new dangers. I wonder if we'll ever be free to live a normal life again."

Jack's heart ached at her words. He thought back to his old life, a life of simplicity on the coast, before the magic of Nalos had swept him away. But he also knew that, deep down, there was no going back. "We'll make it through this," he said softly. "Together."

A Moment of Vulnerability

In the quiet of their cell, Lyria turned to Jack, her expression softer now. "Jack, I've been meaning to ask... What was it like before all of this? Before we met?"

Jack hesitated, the memories of his past flickering in his mind. "I grew up alone for the most part. After my parents died, Charlie raised me, taught me everything I know. But when he passed, I was left with nothing. More alone than ever. That's when I started drifting, looking for something more."

Lyria listened intently, her hand resting gently on his arm. "I can't imagine what that must've been like."

Jack sighed, his voice heavy with emotion. "It was lonely. But I didn't know any different. Then I met you, and everything changed."

Lyria smiled, her eyes shimmering with unshed tears. "I feel the same way. Meeting you was like finding the piece of my soul that had been missing."

For a moment, the tension of their situation faded, replaced by the warmth of their connection. Jack leaned in, pressing a soft kiss to her forehead. "We're going to get out of this, Lyria. I promise."

She nodded, her heart steady with renewed hope. "I trust you."

Preparing for the Abyssal Realm

The next day, as they were led through the stone corridors to the entrance of the Abyssal Realm, Jack and Lyria held onto that hope. Their plan was risky, but it was the only way forward. Together, they would face whatever dangers the underwater world held—and with each passing moment, their bond grew stronger.

The captors believed they controlled the situation, but Jack and Lyria had a plan of their own. And as the Keeper's followers escorted them to the edge of the dark, mysterious waters, they exchanged a glance filled with determination.

Chapter 7: Descent into the Abyssal Realm

Jack and Lyria stood at the edge of the dark, rippling waters that marked the entrance to the Abyssal Realm. The cavernous walls around them loomed tall, and the faint echoes of the Keeper's warning about the perilous journey ahead still hung in the air. The weight of their task pressed heavily on both of them—retrieving the Abyssal Key was their only way to escape this twisted place. But Jack's mind was already plotting beyond that. Could they turn the tables on their captors?

Lyria glanced at Jack, her eyes filled with determination. "Ready?"

Jack nodded, though his heart pounded in his chest. "As ready as I'll ever be."

With that, Lyria stepped toward the water, and as her toes touched the surface, her transformation began. The soft shimmer of magic flowed over her body as her legs fused into a sleek, shimmering tail, her skin glowing with the ethereal light of the sea. She was breathtaking—a true vision of the mythical mermaid she became in the water. Jack felt his breath catch, his love for her deepening with every moment.

She turned back to him, her eyes sparkling. "Hold on tight. The Abyssal Realm isn't like anything you've ever seen."

Without hesitation, Jack grasped her hand, and together they plunged into the cold, dark waters.

The Mysterious Depths of the Abyssal Realm

As they descended beneath the surface, the world around them shifted. The water grew colder, thicker, and a strange, otherworldly glow illuminated the deep sea floor far below. Coral reefs, unlike anything from Jack's world, twisted and spiraled in intricate patterns, their colors so vibrant they almost seemed alive. Schools of glowing fish darted past them, their light illuminating the path forward.

Jack's lungs burned, but Lyria kept him close, pulling him along as they swam deeper into the Abyssal Realm. She moved with grace and ease, her tail propelling them forward at incredible speed. Jack marveled at her strength and beauty in the water, and he felt a sense of awe at this mystical world hidden beneath the waves.

As they approached a massive, ancient structure rising from the ocean floor, Jack felt a strange energy pulsating through the water. "Is that it?" he asked, his voice muffled through the water.

Lyria nodded. "The Temple of the Abyss. The Abyssal Key is inside."

The temple was ancient, its stone walls covered in coral and seaweed, but the energy radiating from it was undeniable.

As they swam closer, they could see the entrance, flanked by two massive stone guardians carved into the shape of sea serpents.

The Challenge of the Abyssal Temple

The entrance to the temple was dark and foreboding, but Jack and Lyria had no choice but to press on. Inside, the temperature dropped even further, and the water felt thicker, as if the temple itself was resisting their presence. Strange symbols lined the walls, glowing faintly with a mysterious blue light.

"This place is ancient," Lyria whispered. "It's said to be guarded by a force more powerful than anything in the ocean. We need to be careful."

As they ventured deeper into the temple, they came across a large chamber. In the center stood a pedestal, and atop it rested the Abyssal Key—a smooth, intricately carved crystal, pulsing with dark energy.

Jack reached for it, but Lyria grabbed his arm. "Wait," she warned. "It won't be that easy."

As if on cue, the water around them began to swirl, and from the shadows emerged a massive creature—a Leviathan. Its body was serpentine, its eyes glowing with malevolent intelligence as it circled them, blocking their path to the key.

"We have to fight it," Lyria said, her voice steady.

Jack drew his sword, though underwater combat wasn't something he was particularly skilled at. Lyria, however, moved with lethal grace, her tail propelling her toward the beast with blinding speed. She slashed at the Leviathan with a dagger she had concealed, but the creature's thick scales deflected the blows.

"We need to distract it," Jack shouted. "I'll draw its attention—go for the key!"

Lyria hesitated for only a second before nodding. "Be careful."

Jack charged at the Leviathan, slashing wildly as it roared in anger. The beast lunged toward him, its jaws snapping dangerously close. Jack barely managed to dodge its attack, but the distraction worked. While the Leviathan was focused on him, Lyria darted toward the pedestal, her movements quick and precise.

She grabbed the Abyssal Key and, as soon as her fingers wrapped around it, a powerful surge of energy rippled through the temple. The Leviathan let out a deafening roar, its massive body convulsing as it was struck by the force of the key's magic.

"Jack, let's go!" Lyria shouted, holding the key tightly in her hand.

Jack didn't need to be told twice. He swam toward her, narrowly avoiding the thrashing tail of the Leviathan as they made their escape from the temple.

Turning the Tables

They emerged from the temple, the Abyssal Key clutched in Lyria's hand. As they swam upward, Jack could feel the weight of their victory, but also the uncertainty of what would come next. The key was powerful—dangerous, even—and they were still in the clutches of their captors.

As they broke the surface of the water and climbed back onto the rocky shore, Lyria transformed back into her human form. She looked at Jack, her expression a mix of relief and determination.

"We have it," Jack said, catching his breath. "Now what?"

Before Lyria could answer, they were surrounded once again by the Keeper's followers. The Keeper himself stepped forward, his masked face unreadable. "You've done well. The Abyssal Key is ours."

Jack narrowed his eyes. "You said if we retrieved the key, you'd let us go."

The Keeper chuckled softly. "I said you would be free—if you survived. And you did."

Lyria stepped forward, holding the key tightly. "But we're not handing it over without something in return. You promised us freedom, but we need more than that."

The Keeper tilted his head. "And what would that be?"

Jack stepped beside Lyria, his heart pounding. "We want information. You said you didn't care about the Heart of

Nalos, but surely you've heard things. We need to find it, and you know something that can help us."

The Keeper paused, his fingers tapping against his cloak. "I've heard whispers, yes. A secret, buried deep within the land of shadows. If you wish to find the Heart, you must seek out the Oracle of Ithara. She is the only one who knows the way."

Jack exchanged a glance with Lyria. The Oracle of Ithara. It was the lead they had been searching for, a glimmer of hope in their quest to reclaim the Heart.

Lyria held out the key. "This is yours. But we want your word that you'll let us leave."

The Keeper's eyes glinted beneath the mask. "You have my word."

Reluctantly, Lyria handed over the Abyssal Key. The Keeper's followers immediately swarmed around him, eagerly examining the ancient artifact. But true to his word, the Keeper signaled for his followers to step aside, allowing Jack and Lyria a clear path to freedom.

A New Path Forward

As they left the cave, the dark atmosphere lifted, and Jack breathed a sigh of relief. They were free—but their journey continued. The Heart of Nalos was still out there, and now they had a new lead. The Oracle of Ithara.

Lyria turned to Jack, her expression softening. "We're getting closer. I can feel it."

Jack nodded, though his thoughts lingered on their recent encounter. The Abyssal Realm had been dangerous, but they had emerged stronger, their bond even more unbreakable. And yet, the shadow of Kaldros still loomed over them, a constant reminder of the danger they faced.

As they walked through the strange, mystical landscape, Jack couldn't help but think about the future. "Lyria," he said softly, "what if... what if we don't ever find the Heart?"

Lyria looked at him, her eyes full of understanding. "We will, Jack. But even if we don't... we have each other. That's enough for me."

Jack smiled, feeling a warmth spread through him. She was right. As long as they were together, they could face anything.

Their journey would continue—through dangers, mysteries, and unknowns—but they were no longer just searching for the Heart of Nalos. They were building something deeper, something more meaningful.

And with the Oracle of Ithara on the horizon, the next chapter of their adventure awaited.

Chapter 8: The Path to Ithara's Oracle

The journey to the Oracle of Ithara had begun, but Jack and Lyria knew that their path would be fraught with dangers and uncertainty. The Keeper's cryptic clues had led them toward the mysterious land of shadows, but no exact location was given. Instead, they were left to follow whispers on the wind, faint traces of ancient knowledge, and their own instincts as they pressed forward.

Though they had survived the Abyssal Realm and defeated their captors, the challenges ahead felt even more daunting. Jack could feel the weight of the quest growing heavier, the stakes higher, as they ventured into unknown territories. And yet, through it all, the bond between him and Lyria continued to deepen. The love that had blossomed between them was no longer just a spark—it had grown into a roaring flame.

They set off across the rolling hills and enchanted forests that surrounded the Keeper's domain, determined to find the Oracle, even if it meant facing new and unknown threats.

An Unseen Force Guides Them

For days, they wandered through the mystical lands, following only the vaguest sense of direction. The landscape around them was ever-shifting—one moment, they were walking through a forest of trees with glowing blue leaves, and the next, they found themselves crossing a field of golden sands beneath a crimson sky. Time seemed to behave differently here, making it impossible to know how long they had been traveling.

"Do you think we're even on the right path?" Jack asked, frustration creeping into his voice as they stopped to rest by a crystal-clear stream.

Lyria sat beside him, her shimmering hair catching the strange light of the world around them. "I don't know," she admitted. "But I feel something guiding us, like a force beyond our understanding. Ithara's Oracle is ancient—perhaps it wants us to find her, but it won't make it easy."

Jack nodded, though doubt gnawed at him. "It's just that we've been walking for what feels like weeks, and we're no closer to finding her than we were when we started."

Lyria smiled softly and reached for his hand. "That's what makes this an adventure, Jack. The unknown. And besides..." Her voice dropped to a teasing whisper. "I'd rather be wandering in this strange world with you than anywhere else."

Jack's heart swelled at her words, and he found himself smiling despite the weight of their mission. "You always know how to make me feel better," he said, his tone light.

She leaned in closer. "It's because we're in this together. No matter what happens."

A Dangerous Encounter in the Forest of Whispers

Their journey continued, but as they ventured deeper into a dense, overgrown forest known only as the Forest of Whispers, the sense of foreboding grew stronger. The trees here were twisted, their branches reaching out like skeletal fingers. Strange whispers echoed through the air, though no source of the voices could be seen.

"It's not safe here," Lyria said, her voice barely audible above the eerie murmurs of the forest.

Jack's hand instinctively moved to the hilt of his sword. "What's causing those whispers?"

Lyria shook her head. "I don't know, but I've heard stories of this place. It's said that the forest is alive—that it can sense the thoughts and fears of those who pass through it."

As they pushed forward, the whispers grew louder, more insistent. Jack could hear faint voices calling his name, speaking of his past, of the losses he had endured. The memories of his parents' tragic deaths and the years spent alone with the old fisherman flooded his mind. He tried to shake them off, but the forest seemed to feed on his pain.

Lyria, too, appeared affected by the whispers. Her face was pale, her eyes distant, as if the forest was pulling her into memories of her own. "We need to keep moving," she urged, though her voice wavered.

Suddenly, the trees parted, revealing a dark, shadowy figure standing in their path. It was cloaked in darkness, its form shifting like smoke. The whispers grew deafening, and Jack could feel a chill run down his spine.

"Who are you?" Jack demanded, gripping his sword.

The figure did not respond with words. Instead, it extended a hand, and a cold wind swept through the forest. Jack's breath caught in his throat as he felt a force pulling him toward the shadow, like an invisible hand tugging at his very soul.

"Jack!" Lyria's voice cut through the noise, breaking the spell. She grabbed his arm and pulled him back, her strength anchoring him to reality.

The shadowy figure seemed to hesitate, then vanished as quickly as it had appeared, leaving behind only the fading whispers of the forest.

The Secrets of the Forgotten Temple

Shaken but unharmed, Jack and Lyria hurried through the forest until they reached the edge, where the trees gave way to a vast plain. In the distance, they saw a crumbling structure—a forgotten temple, its stone walls half-buried in the earth.

"Ithara's Oracle must be inside," Jack said, though he knew it was more wishful thinking than certainty.

Lyria frowned. "I don't think so. This temple looks ancient, but I sense something… different about it. We should be cautious."

As they approached the temple, the air around them grew thick with magic. Strange symbols were etched into the stone, glowing faintly in the dim light. The doors to the temple were ajar, and a soft hum emanated from within, like the sound of distant chanting.

Jack and Lyria exchanged a glance before stepping inside.

The temple's interior was unlike anything Jack had ever seen. The walls were covered in murals depicting long-forgotten gods and ancient battles. At the center of the room stood a pedestal, and on it rested an ornate stone tablet.

Lyria's eyes widened as she studied the tablet. "This is a relic from the time of the Old Gods," she whispered. "It's said that those who can decipher its runes will unlock the secrets of the universe."

Jack approached the pedestal, his curiosity piqued. "Do you think it could help us find the Oracle?"

"I don't know," Lyria said, her brow furrowed. "But it's worth a try."

As they examined the tablet, a low rumble echoed through the temple, and the ground beneath their feet began to shake. Jack's hand instinctively went to his sword as cracks spread across the floor.

"We need to get out of here," he said urgently, grabbing Lyria's hand.

But before they could make it to the exit, the ground gave way, and they fell into the darkness below.

Trapped in the Underground Maze

Jack groaned as he hit the cold, hard ground. His head throbbed, and it took him a moment to regain his bearings. They had fallen into an underground chamber—a maze of twisting tunnels that seemed to stretch endlessly in every direction.

Lyria stirred beside him, wincing as she sat up. "Where are we?"

"I don't know," Jack replied, his voice tight with frustration. "But it looks like we're trapped."

The walls of the tunnel were made of dark, smooth stone, and the air was thick with a damp, musty smell. Strange markings covered the walls, similar to the ones they had seen in the temple above.

"We need to find a way out," Lyria said, her voice steady despite the dire situation.

Together, they began to navigate the maze, but it quickly became apparent that the tunnels were designed to disorient and confuse. Every turn led them deeper into the labyrinth, and soon, Jack lost all sense of direction.

"We could be down here for days," Jack muttered, his frustration growing.

Lyria placed a hand on his arm, calming him. "We'll find a way out. We've faced worse than this."

Jack nodded, though he couldn't shake the feeling of dread that had settled in his chest. The maze seemed to be playing tricks on his mind—whispers echoed in the distance, and every so often, he caught glimpses of shadowy figures lurking just beyond the edge of his vision.

After what felt like hours of wandering, they stumbled upon a chamber that was different from the rest. At the center of the room stood a massive, intricately carved door, covered in the same runes they had seen earlier.

"This must be the way out," Jack said, his voice filled with hope.

Lyria studied the runes carefully. "It's a puzzle," she said, her brow furrowed. "We need to decipher the symbols to unlock the door."

Jack's heart sank. "Do you think you can figure it out?"

Lyria smiled, though there was a hint of exhaustion in her eyes. "I'll try."

As Lyria worked on the puzzle, Jack's mind began to wander. His thoughts drifted back to his old life—the one he had left behind. The memories were distant now, but the pain of losing his parents still lingered, like an old wound that had never fully healed.

"Lyria," he said softly, "have you ever wondered what life would have been like if we hadn't come to this place? If we were just... normal?"

Lyria paused, glancing up at him. "I have," she admitted. "But then I think about everything we've experienced together. And I realize that, no matter how difficult it's been, I wouldn't trade it for anything."

Before Jack could respond, there was a soft click, and the door in front of them slowly began to creak open. Lyria had solved the puzzle.

"Let's go," she said, her voice filled with determination.

The Journey Continues

The door led them out of the underground maze and back into the strange, mystical world above. Though they were no closer to finding the Oracle of Ithara, they had overcome yet another obstacle.

As they stepped into the open air, Jack took a deep breath, feeling the tension in his chest begin to ease. They were still far from their goal, but with Lyria by his side, he knew they could face whatever came next.

The Oracle was out there—waiting for them. And they wouldn't stop until they found her.

Chapter 9: Encounters with the Absurd

The endless journey to find the Oracle of Ithara stretched on, with Jack and Lyria wandering through increasingly mystical and absurd landscapes. Their pursuit of the Oracle, the only one who could lead them to the missing Heart of Nalos, had grown more complicated than they could have imagined. Yet, the spark of determination in both their hearts kept them moving forward.

As the sun began to set on the strange horizon—where trees glowed in a multitude of colors, and clouds swirled with patterns like paintings in the sky—Jack and Lyria found themselves standing at the edge of a dense and twisted forest. The trees here bent and swayed unnaturally, their branches knotting together like tangled hair.

Jack held Lyria's hand as they peered into the gloom of the woods. "Does this feel right to you? Something about this place... it's strange."

Lyria, who had learned to trust the magic that flowed within her mermaid blood, tilted her head and listened to the forest. "I think this place is more than it appears," she murmured. "There's something inside calling us. But not the Oracle—something else."

Jack gripped his sword tighter, nodding. "Let's be ready for anything."

An Unlikely Encounter in the Twisted Forest

As they ventured deeper into the forest, the sounds of their footsteps were muffled by thick moss, and the branches above seemed to close in on them like a cage. The air was thick with the scent of damp earth and something faintly sweet, like forgotten memories.

Without warning, the ground beneath them shifted, and Jack and Lyria stumbled. Roots shot up from the soil, coiling around their feet like serpents. Jack unsheathed his sword, ready to strike, but Lyria placed a calming hand on his arm.

"Wait," she whispered. "Look."

From between the trees emerged two figures, their forms shifting in the shadows. As they came into the light, Jack couldn't help but raise an eyebrow. One of them was an enormously tall man, towering nearly ten feet, with a beard made entirely of golden feathers. His eyes were wide and owl-like, glowing in the dim light. Beside him was a short, round woman with an astonishingly high-pitched voice. Her entire body seemed to shimmer as if covered in fish scales, though she was no mermaid. Instead, her clothes sparkled with small gemstones that jingled like wind chimes when she moved.

"Who are you?" Jack asked, his grip on the sword not loosening just yet.

The tall man stepped forward, his voice slow and deep, like distant thunder. "We are the Keepers of the Forgotten."

The round woman spoke next, her voice unnervingly fast. "But we're not here to stop you! No, no, not at all. We need your help!"

Jack and Lyria exchanged a glance. "Our help?" Lyria asked.

The Keepers nodded vigorously. The tall man bent low to meet Jack's eyes. "Yes. We are bound to this forest by ancient magic. Our freedom can only be granted if someone helps us recover something that was stolen from us long ago."

Jack sighed inwardly. More detours, more quests. It seemed like every step toward the Oracle was interrupted by yet another strange twist. But Lyria, ever kind-hearted, stepped forward, her voice soft and warm.

"What was stolen from you?" she asked.

The woman twirled on her toes, the gems on her dress tinkling like bells. "A prized possession! A key of sorts, you see. It opens the way to something powerful. But without it, we're trapped here, in this endless, shifting forest."

Jack frowned. "And if we help you get it back?"

The tall man smiled, his feathered beard fluttering in the breeze. "We will grant you a reward—one that will help you in your quest."

Jack and Lyria were quiet for a moment, considering the offer. They needed every advantage they could get if they were ever going to find the Oracle and, ultimately, the Heart of Nalos.

"We'll help," Jack said at last, his tone firm.

Lyria squeezed his hand in agreement. "Tell us where to find this key."

A Dangerous Expedition to the Mountains of Echoes

The Keepers directed Jack and Lyria toward the Mountains of Echoes, a range that lay just beyond the twisted forest. According to the Keepers, the key was hidden deep within a cave at the mountain's peak, guarded by strange and unpredictable creatures known as the Echo Shades.

As they trekked toward the mountains, Lyria stayed close to Jack, the gentle brush of her hand against his arm sending warmth through him. Though their journey had been long and perilous, Jack couldn't help but feel at peace whenever she was near. The adventures had brought them closer, and the subtle touches, shared glances, and scattered kisses told Jack that they were no longer just companions—they were bound by something far deeper.

Halfway up the mountain, they paused to catch their breath. Jack looked out at the horizon, the twisted forest now a distant shadow below. He turned to Lyria, who was sitting on a nearby rock, gazing into the distance.

"Lyria," Jack began, his voice hesitant, "we've talked so much about my past, but you've never told me much about yours."

Lyria smiled faintly, her sea-green eyes softening. "I suppose it's time I tell you the truth."

Jack sat beside her, listening intently.

"My parents… they're not gone. At least, I don't think they are. They disappeared a long time ago, leaving me behind in the ocean. I've searched for them ever since, but I've never found any trace of where they went. Some say they were taken by a powerful force, something ancient and hidden deep within the seas."

Jack reached out, placing his hand over hers. "Do you think they're still out there?"

Lyria's voice trembled slightly as she spoke. "I hope so. Every time I dive beneath the waves, I feel them, like a distant song calling to me. That's why I've never given up."

Jack squeezed her hand, his heart aching for her. "We'll find them, Lyria. Just like we'll find the Oracle. I promise."

She turned to him, her eyes shimmering with gratitude. Without a word, she leaned in and kissed him softly, the connection between them deepening with each passing moment.

Facing the Echo Shades

Their conversation was cut short as they approached the mouth of the cave, the entrance to the lair of the Echo Shades. The air around them grew colder, and the sound of wind whistling through the rocks created an eerie melody.

"They're inside," Lyria whispered, drawing closer to Jack. "Be ready."

Jack nodded, drawing his sword as they entered the cave. The walls were smooth and dark, reflecting the faint light of their torches. But as they moved deeper into the cave, the shadows around them began to shift unnervingly.

Suddenly, a cold breeze swept through the cave, and from the darkness emerged the Echo Shades—shadowy creatures with elongated limbs and hollow, echoing voices. Their forms shimmered and rippled like smoke, making it difficult to tell where they were.

"Stay close," Jack muttered, raising his sword as the creatures circled them.

The Echo Shades moved swiftly, darting in and out of the darkness, their laughter echoing eerily. One of them lunged at Jack, its clawed hand swiping through the air. He barely managed to block the strike, the force of it sending him stumbling backward.

Lyria moved with grace and agility, her mermaid powers lending her strength even on land. She summoned the magic of the sea, sending a wave of water crashing into the creatures, slowing their movements.

"They're trying to confuse us," Jack called out, swinging his sword at another Shade that appeared beside him.

The battle was long and intense, the Echo Shades' laughter filling the cave as they toyed with Jack and Lyria. But with each passing moment, the couple's coordination grew stronger. They fought together as one, moving in perfect harmony, their connection unspoken but undeniable.

Finally, after what felt like an eternity, the last of the Echo Shades dissolved into the shadows, and the cave fell silent.

Lyria breathed a sigh of relief, wiping the sweat from her brow. "That was too close."

Jack smiled wearily, sheathing his sword. "At least we made it through."

They continued deeper into the cave until they found a small chamber at the very end. In the center of the room sat a pedestal, and resting atop it was a small, ornate key that glowed faintly in the dim light.

"The key," Jack said, his voice filled with relief.

Lyria reached out and took the key, holding it up to examine it. "This is what the Keepers were searching for."

Jack nodded. "Let's get back to them."

A Priceless Reward

When they returned to the Keepers of the Forgotten, the two strange figures greeted them with wide smiles. The tall man's feathered beard quivered with excitement, while the short woman twirled on her toes in delight.

"You found it!" the woman squealed, clapping her hands.

Jack handed the key to the Keepers, who held it reverently. "We kept our end of the bargain," he said. "Now it's your turn."

The tall man nodded solemnly. "You have done us a great service. As promised, we will give you something to aid you on your journey."

From within his robes, the man produced a small, glowing orb. "This is a beacon," he explained. "It will guide you through the misty paths and hidden places of this world. When you are lost, follow its light, and it will lead you to the Oracle of Ithara."

Lyria's eyes widened. "This will help us find her."

The round woman nodded. "Indeed. The Oracle's location is ever-changing, but this beacon will show you the way."

Jack accepted the orb, feeling its warmth in his hands. "Thank you."

With their new prize in hand and their bond stronger than ever, Jack and Lyria prepared for the next leg of their journey. The Oracle was still out there, waiting for them. But now, they had something more—a beacon of hope that would light their way through the darkness ahead.

Chapter 10: The Climb to the Oracle

Jack and Lyria stood at the base of another towering mountain, this one even more imposing and surreal than the last. Clouds swirled around its jagged peaks, obscuring the summit. They had left behind the twisted forest and its strange Keepers with the beacon orb now glowing faintly in Jack's hand.

The Oracle of Ithara was close, yet the path ahead was far from straightforward. Each step took them deeper into the mysterious island, where magic and danger entwined with every breath of the wind.

The Orb's Guidance

Jack held the glowing orb before him, its light flickering in response to their surroundings. It pulsed like a heartbeat, seemingly in tune with the island itself. The path ahead twisted up the mountainside, disappearing into a mist that clung to the rocks like a veil.

Lyria, ever alert, studied the orb's rhythm. "It's leading us upward," she said softly. "The Oracle must be somewhere high in the mountains."

Jack nodded. "Let's hope we don't run into anything like the Echo Shades this time."

They had barely recovered from their battle in the cave, but both knew there was no time to rest. The Oracle was their only hope of finding the Heart of Nalos, and with every delay, they risked the artifact falling into Kaldros's hands.

Together, they began their ascent, their movements in sync as they navigated the narrow, treacherous path. The orb's light illuminated their way, casting eerie shadows on the jagged rocks surrounding them. The air grew thinner the higher they climbed, and the temperature dropped, but neither Jack nor Lyria slowed their pace.

The Mystical Beasts of the Mountain

As they climbed, the landscape shifted from rocky cliffs to something more ethereal. The plants grew stranger, their leaves iridescent and glowing faintly in the dim light. Some trees seemed to hum with a low, melodic vibration, while others twisted in unnatural spirals toward the sky. There was something alive about the mountain itself, as though it pulsed with a hidden energy.

Then, the first sign of trouble appeared.

Ahead of them, blocking the narrow path, stood a massive creature unlike anything Jack had ever seen. It was as tall as two men, with the body of a lion and the head of a great bird. Its feathers were a shimmering gold, and its eyes burned with a deep, unnatural intelligence.

Lyria gasped softly, gripping Jack's arm. "A Gryndor," she whispered. "I've only heard stories about them. They guard places of great power."

The creature's golden eyes fixed on them, unblinking. Jack tightened his hold on his sword, but Lyria stepped forward.

"No," she said gently, "we don't fight this one."

Jack hesitated, unsure. "Then what do we do?"

Lyria's voice was steady. "Gryndors are drawn to music. We have to offer it something in harmony with the mountain's magic."

Her hand reached out to touch a nearby tree, and Jack watched in awe as the tree began to hum, vibrating in response to her touch. Lyria closed her eyes, her voice rising in a soft, lilting song that seemed to blend with the mountain's melody.

The Gryndor tilted its head, listening intently. Its fierce gaze softened, and slowly, it stepped aside, allowing them to pass.

Jack exhaled in relief, his heart still pounding. "That was... incredible."

Lyria smiled at him, her cheeks flushed from the effort. "It's all part of this world. You just have to know how to listen."

They continued their ascent, but Jack couldn't shake the growing sense that they were heading deeper into a place where the laws of reality no longer applied. The creatures of the island were becoming more bizarre, more unpredictable.

They had passed the realm of the familiar and were now
fully immersed in the absurdity of the island's magic.

A Dangerous Climb

Hours passed as they climbed higher and higher, the orb's
light guiding them through the swirling mist. The path
became more treacherous, with narrow ledges and steep
drops on either side. Jack led the way, his sword at the
ready, while Lyria kept her eyes on the orb, ensuring they
were following its glow.

Suddenly, the ground beneath them shifted, and Jack felt his
foot slip on the loose gravel. He reached out, grabbing hold
of a jagged rock to steady himself, but the rock gave way,
and he nearly tumbled over the edge. Lyria was there in an
instant, her hand gripping his tightly as she pulled him back
to safety.

"Careful," she whispered, her eyes wide with concern.

Jack nodded, his breath coming in ragged gasps. "Thanks."

The mountain seemed to grow more malevolent as they
neared the top. Strange winds whipped around them,
carrying whispers that neither could understand. The sky
above darkened, and distant lightning flashed, though there
was no thunder to accompany it.

Lyria shivered as they pressed onward. "It feels like the
mountain is alive, testing us."

Jack didn't disagree. There was something deeply unsettling about the place, as though it resented their presence.

The Cave of the Oracle

At long last, they reached a plateau near the summit, where a massive cave entrance yawned before them. The orb's glow grew brighter, pulsing rapidly in Jack's hand. They had arrived at the cave where the Oracle of Ithara was said to dwell.

The entrance was flanked by statues of strange creatures—half-human, half-serpent beings with wings folded across their bodies. Their eyes seemed to follow Jack and Lyria as they approached, and the air was thick with an ancient, almost oppressive magic.

Jack took a deep breath, steeling himself. "This is it."

Lyria nodded, her face serious. "Be ready for anything."

They stepped inside, the cave's interior dark and echoing. The walls were smooth, as though carved by some unseen force, and the air was cold and damp. The orb's light flickered, casting long shadows on the walls.

The deeper they ventured into the cave, the more intense the magic became. Jack could feel it buzzing in the air, a sensation that made the hair on the back of his neck stand on end. It was as if the very rocks around them were alive, watching their every move.

And then, they heard it—a soft, melodic voice, coming from deeper within the cave.

"That must be the Oracle," Jack said, his voice hushed.

But as they rounded the corner, they were met with a sight they hadn't expected.

The Oracle's Guardians

Instead of the Oracle, they found themselves face to face with another set of creatures—this time, two enormous serpentine beings with glowing eyes and scales that shimmered like liquid silver. They coiled around the entrance to a smaller chamber, blocking the way forward.

Jack tightened his grip on his sword, but Lyria held up a hand. "Wait," she said. "They're guarding the Oracle."

The serpents hissed softly, their eyes narrowing as they watched Jack and Lyria closely. It was clear they weren't going to let them pass without a challenge.

"What do we do?" Jack asked, his voice low.

Lyria frowned, her mind racing. "There has to be something—some way to prove we're worthy."

The serpents' eyes flickered, and Jack noticed something strange: one of the creatures had a small, golden charm wrapped around its neck, glowing faintly in the dim light. It was shaped like a key.

"That charm," Jack said, pointing. "It's connected to the Oracle somehow."

Lyria's eyes widened as she realized what he was saying. "We have to retrieve it."

Jack nodded. "But how?"

Before they could come up with a plan, the serpents began to move, their massive bodies shifting as they slithered toward Jack and Lyria. The ground shook beneath their weight, and Jack raised his sword, ready for battle.

But Lyria, quick as ever, darted forward, her hands glowing with a soft blue light. She called upon the magic of the ocean, summoning a wave of water that surged toward the serpents, momentarily distracting them.

"Now, Jack!" she called.

Without hesitation, Jack lunged forward, his sword slicing through the air. He reached for the golden charm, his fingers closing around it just as the serpent snapped at him with its fangs. He rolled to the side, narrowly avoiding its strike, and held up the charm triumphantly.

The serpents hissed, their eyes narrowing, but they didn't attack again. Instead, they slithered back to their original positions, watching Jack and Lyria with an unsettling calm.

A New Ally for the Journey Ahead

With the charm in hand, Jack and Lyria stepped forward into the inner chamber, where a soft light glowed from within. The air grew warmer, and the magic in the cave intensified. The Oracle had to be close.

But before they could move any further, they were interrupted by a voice.

"Well, well, well… look what we have here."

Jack and Lyria whirled around to find themselves face to face with a new figure—a man dressed in flowing robes, his face obscured by a hood. His eyes gleamed with mischief, and he held a staff that crackled with energy.

"Who are you?" Jack demanded, his sword still raised.

The man chuckled softly. "A friend, perhaps. Or an enemy. It all depends on what you seek."

Lyria frowned. "We seek the Oracle of Ithara."

The man's smile widened. "Of course you do. But you're not the only ones."

Jack exchanged a worried glance with Lyria. The Oracle was still out of reach, and now, they had another obstacle in their path.

Chapter 11: The Path to the Oracle

The cave's cold air clung to Jack's skin as he and Lyria ventured deeper into the mysterious mountain. The golden charm they had retrieved from the serpents glowed faintly in his hand, its warmth pulsing in rhythm with their steps. Each moment they drew closer to the Oracle, the island's magic grew more intense, and the shadows around them seemed to shift and pulse with life. Yet they knew this was just the beginning. Finding the Oracle was the next step in uncovering the location of the Heart of Nalos, but the obstacles ahead were becoming increasingly perilous.

The Mystical Maze of the Mountain

The further they went, the narrower the path became, until the rocky walls of the cave seemed to close in around them. Strange markings appeared on the stone, glowing faintly with ancient magic. Jack paused to study one of them, recognizing the symbols from his studies with Lyria's help. They were ancient runes, possibly tied to the Oracle's magic.

"These symbols," Lyria whispered, running her fingers over them. "They're warnings. This mountain was designed to keep intruders away."

Jack's grip tightened on his sword. "Well, it's doing a good job of that."

Suddenly, the ground beneath them began to shift. A deep rumble echoed through the cave, and before they could react, the floor split open. The rocks gave way, and both Jack and Lyria tumbled down into the darkness.

They fell for what felt like an eternity, the cold wind rushing past them. Jack's heart raced as he tried to grab hold of anything to stop their descent, but there was nothing but empty air. Just as panic began to set in, they hit a slope and slid down through a tunnel, finally landing in a strange, cavernous chamber.

The room was enormous, the ceiling so high it disappeared into the shadows. Strange glowing crystals jutted out of the walls, casting an eerie blue light over the space. In the center of the room stood a massive stone structure, its surface covered in more ancient runes.

"Where are we?" Jack asked, getting to his feet and helping Lyria up.

Lyria's eyes scanned the chamber, her brow furrowed in concentration. "It's a maze," she said quietly. "A magical labyrinth designed to test anyone who seeks the Oracle."

Jack looked around, feeling the weight of the challenge ahead. "Great. So how do we get through it?"

Lyria's gaze locked on the stone structure in the center of the room. "We have to unlock the runes," she said. "Each one is a clue. If we solve them, the path to the Oracle will open."

Deciphering the Runes

The glowing runes pulsed with a soft, hypnotic light, beckoning Jack and Lyria closer. Jack knelt in front of the massive stone and studied the symbols, trying to make sense of their ancient meaning. Lyria crouched beside him, her fingers brushing over the surface of the stone as she murmured softly to herself.

"These runes are different from the ones we've seen before," Lyria said, her voice thoughtful. "They're more complex. Each one represents a challenge."

Jack's brow furrowed. "Challenges like...?"

Before Lyria could answer, the air around them shifted, and the ground trembled beneath their feet. The runes on the stone flared to life, glowing brightly as the room transformed around them. The walls began to move, shifting and reshaping themselves into towering stone columns and jagged cliffs. A thick fog rolled in, obscuring their view and turning the room into a surreal, ever-changing landscape.

"We've triggered the first test," Lyria said, her voice steady despite the chaos around them.

Jack's heart pounded in his chest as he drew his sword. "What now?"

Lyria smiled faintly, her eyes glinting with determination. "We solve the puzzle."

The first rune, glowing a deep red, was etched into a stone pillar that had risen out of the ground. Jack approached it cautiously, studying the intricate design. The rune seemed to pulse in time with the heartbeat of the island, its energy crackling through the air.

"There's something familiar about this," Jack muttered.

Lyria joined him, her gaze thoughtful. "It's a fire rune," she said. "It represents heat, destruction... and rebirth."

Jack's eyes flickered with understanding. "We need to summon fire."

Before either of them could act, the fog thickened, and from the shadows emerged a pack of flame-wreathed beasts. Their eyes glowed like embers, and their breath came out in waves of heat.

"We fight," Jack said, gripping his sword tightly. The beasts circled around them, their fiery bodies casting long, flickering shadows across the stone walls.

Lyria stepped back, her hands glowing with blue energy as she prepared her magic. "Ready when you are."

The Battle of Flames

The first beast lunged at Jack, its fiery maw snapping inches from his face. Jack ducked and slashed his sword across its side, the blade cutting through the flames as though slicing through air. The creature roared in pain, but it didn't falter. Instead, it seemed to grow stronger, its flames intensifying.

"Careful!" Lyria warned. "They feed on energy!"

Jack gritted his teeth as another beast lunged at him. This time, instead of attacking, he sidestepped the creature, letting it crash into one of the stone pillars. The impact caused the rune on the pillar to flare up, sending a shockwave of heat through the room.

The beasts recoiled, their flames flickering as the rune absorbed their energy.

"That's it!" Lyria shouted, her voice ringing with realization. "We need to use the runes to draw their power away."

Jack nodded, his eyes sharp with determination. He ducked and weaved through the pack of beasts, guiding them toward the pillars. Each time one of the creatures made contact with a rune, the flames dimmed, and the beasts grew weaker.

Lyria, using her water magic, summoned waves of cool mist that doused the flames around them. The combination of their attacks weakened the beasts further until finally, the last of them collapsed, its fiery body dissolving into ash.

As the final beast fell, the rune on the central stone flared brightly before dimming to a soft glow. The room shifted again, the fog dissipating as the stone pillars sank back into the ground.

"We did it," Jack said, panting as he wiped sweat from his brow.

Lyria smiled, her eyes gleaming with triumph. "One down. Let's hope the next one is easier."

The Cold Test

The second rune, a cool, frosty blue, appeared on a different pillar. Jack and Lyria approached it cautiously, wary of what challenge lay ahead. This time, the air around them grew colder, and frost began to creep along the ground. The warmth of the cave was replaced by an icy chill that sank into their bones.

"Cold," Lyria murmured. "This test is about endurance."

Before Jack could respond, the ground beneath them rumbled again, and from the frost-covered walls emerged towering ice golems. Their bodies were made of solid ice, their movements slow but deliberate. Each step they took sent tremors through the cave, and their frosty breath crystallized in the air.

"Endurance, huh?" Jack muttered, gripping his sword tightly. "Great."

The golems moved toward them with slow, methodical steps, their massive fists raised to strike. Jack swung his sword, but it glanced off the golem's icy body, barely leaving a scratch.

"We need to melt them," Lyria said, her breath visible in the cold air. She raised her hands, summoning a burst of heat magic that sent a wave of warmth toward the nearest golem. The ice creature hissed as the magic hit it, melting part of its body.

Jack followed her lead, using his sword to chip away at the weakened parts of the golems' bodies. The creatures were slow, but their strength was undeniable. One wrong move, and either Jack or Lyria could be crushed beneath their massive fists.

As they fought, the temperature continued to drop, the cold seeping into their skin and making it harder to move. Jack's breaths came in shallow gasps as he dodged another strike from one of the golems.

"We have to hurry," he said through chattering teeth.

Lyria nodded, her movements becoming more sluggish as the cold took its toll. She summoned another burst of heat magic, this time focusing all her energy on the central golem. The ice around its body began to crack, and with a final burst of power, the creature shattered into a million shards.

With the defeat of the central golem, the cold began to recede, and the second rune dimmed to a soft glow.

"Two down," Lyria said, her voice strained. "But I don't know how much more we can take."

Jack nodded, his breath coming in heavy gasps. "We'll make it," he said, though even he wasn't sure.

The Final Trial

The third rune, glowing a deep purple, appeared on the final pillar. Jack and Lyria approached it cautiously, both of them weary from the previous tests. The air around them seemed to crackle with energy, and the ground beneath their feet trembled.

"This is it," Lyria said softly. "The last trial."

Jack nodded, his eyes fixed on the rune. "Let's finish this."

As soon as they touched the rune, the cave around them shifted one last time. The ground gave way beneath their feet, and they fell into a swirling vortex of energy, the colors around them blending into a mixture of light. For a moment, Jack felt as though he was weightless, suspended in a dimension where time didn't exist.

Then, they landed on solid ground. The vortex faded, and they found themselves in a dark void, the air thick with tension. In front of them stood a massive creature cloaked in shadows, its eyes glowing like twin suns. It was a being of pure energy, its form shifting and flowing like a stream of liquid light.

"Who dares enter the realm of the Oracle?" the creature boomed, its voice echoing through the darkness.

Jack stepped forward, his heart racing. "We seek the Oracle. We have come to learn the location of the Heart of Nalos."

The creature laughed, a sound that sent chills down Jack's spine. "Many have sought the Oracle, but few have proven worthy. To find the Oracle, you must first confront your deepest fears."

A swirling mist enveloped them, and Jack felt his stomach drop as visions of his past flooded his mind. He saw his parents' accident, the wreckage, and the haunting memory of being left alone in the world. The pain of loss and loneliness overwhelmed him, and he stumbled back.

"Jack!" Lyria reached out to him, her voice breaking through the fog. "You can't give in!"

With her encouragement, Jack closed his eyes and focused on the warmth of their bond, the love that had grown between them throughout their journey. He felt Lyria's presence beside him, her magic intertwining with his own. Together, they pushed back against the darkness, confronting their fears.

As they faced the shadows, the swirling mist began to dissipate, revealing the creature before them once more.

"You are stronger than I anticipated," it said, its voice softer now. "Very well. You may seek the Oracle."

With a wave of its hand, the darkness faded, and the room transformed. Jack and Lyria found themselves standing at the entrance to a grand chamber, its walls adorned with shimmering crystals that reflected the light like a million stars.

The Oracle Awaits

They stepped inside, their hearts racing as they approached the center of the chamber. There, on a pedestal, rested a shimmering orb that pulsed with energy. Its surface rippled with the colors of the cosmos.

As they reached for it, a figure emerged from the shadows—a majestic being with silver hair and eyes that sparkled like gemstones. The Oracle was breathtaking, radiating an aura of wisdom and power.

"Welcome, seekers," the Oracle said, his voice melodic and soothing. "I have awaited your arrival."

Jack and Lyria exchanged a glance, their hearts racing with anticipation.

"We've come to learn the location of the Heart of Nalos," Lyria said, her voice steady.

The Oracle smiled, his gaze piercing yet warm. "The Heart is a powerful artifact, and its location is hidden from those who seek it for selfish reasons. But you, children of destiny, have proven your worth."

As the Oracle spoke, the air around them crackled with energy, and the orb began to glow brighter, illuminating the entire chamber.

"However, there's more to your journey," the Oracle continued. "You must prepare yourselves for the trials that lie ahead, for Kaldros is searching for the Heart as well."

Jack's heart sank. "Kaldros? But we've defeated him before!"

The Oracle nodded. "He will stop at nothing to claim the Heart for himself. Your path will be fraught with danger, but you will not face it alone."

Suddenly, the chamber began to shake, and Jack and Lyria exchanged worried glances. The Oracle held up a hand, calming the vibrations.

"The Heart of Nalos is closer than you think," it said. "But you must first complete the final trials and face Kaldros in the Abyssal Realm."

Jack took a deep breath, determination flooding through him. "We will do whatever it takes."

A New Beginning

As the Oracle's words settled in, Jack felt a new sense of purpose washing over him. Lyria stood beside him, her hand finding his, their fingers intertwining as they prepared for the next phase of their journey.

With newfound resolve, they stepped forward, ready to embrace the trials that awaited them. The challenges they had faced had only strengthened their bond, and together, they would confront whatever lay ahead.

As the chamber faded around them, a brilliant light enveloped Jack and Lyria. With the Oracle's guidance, they were one step closer to discovering the Heart of Nalos, and

their love would be their greatest strength in the trials to
come.

Chapter 12: The Abyssal Challenge

Preparing for the Abyssal Realm

As Jack and Lyria stood in the radiant chamber of the Oracle, anticipation thrummed in the air. The Oracle's words echoed in Jack's mind, urging them to prepare for the trials that awaited in the Abyssal Realm. Kaldros was a looming threat, a shadow that danced just out of reach, and the thought of confronting him sent a shiver down Jack's spine.

"We're really doing this," Jack said, gripping Lyria's hand tightly. He searched her eyes for reassurance. "Are we ready for Kaldros?"

Lyria nodded, her expression a blend of determination and confidence. "We are. Together, we can face him."

The Oracle had provided them with a way back to the Abyssal Realm—a shimmering portal that pulsed with energy. Jack took a deep breath, trying to calm the anxiety swirling within him. As they stepped toward the portal, Lyria turned to him, her expression serious.

"Jack, there's something important you need to understand before we dive back into the Abyssal Realm," she said, her voice steady.

"What is it?" Jack asked, furrowing his brow.

"You'll be able to breathe underwater because of me. When we're submerged, the magic between us allows you to draw in the water as air. But if we get separated..." Her voice trailed off, and Jack could see the concern in her eyes.

Jack's stomach dropped. "If we get separated, I won't be able to breathe?"

Lyria nodded, the weight of her words settling heavily between them. "Yes. You'll need to stay close to me. The magic that allows you to survive is tied to my presence."

"I understand," he said, determination flooding his veins. "I won't leave your side."

"Good," Lyria replied, her lips curving into a reassuring smile. "Let's go."

With that, they plunged into the shimmering portal, the world around them dissolving into a swirl of light and color. When they emerged on the other side, the familiar dark waters of the Abyssal Realm enveloped them, and Jack instinctively reached for Lyria, feeling the warmth of her hand in his.

Into the Deep

The moment they submerged, the pressure of the water pressed against Jack, but it didn't suffocate him as it should have. Instead, he felt a sense of weightlessness, as if he were floating through the water. It was disorienting but exhilarating.

As they began to swim deeper into the Abyssal Realm, the surroundings shifted from the tranquil blues of the surface to a rich tapestry of colors illuminated by bioluminescent creatures. Strange fish darted around them, their scales glimmering like jewels in the dim light, and the eerie beauty of the underwater world captivated Jack.

"Look at that!" he exclaimed, pointing to a group of vibrant jellyfish that pulsed in unison, casting a soft glow through the water. "It's incredible!"

Lyria smiled, her eyes sparkling with delight. "The Abyssal Realm is full of wonders. But we must stay focused on our mission."

Jack nodded, his excitement tempered by the reality of their quest. Kaldros lurked somewhere in this mystical underwater world, and they needed to confront him.

As they swam further, Jack felt a strange tug in the water, as if an unseen current was pulling them in a specific direction. "Do you feel that?" he asked.

"Yes," Lyria replied, her expression shifting to one of concentration. "It feels like the heart of the Abyssal Realm is calling us."

Jack could see it now—a faint light glowing in the distance, pulsing like a heartbeat. "Let's go."

The Meeting with Kaldros

They swam toward the light, their hearts pounding with anticipation. As they drew closer, the water around them began to darken, and a foreboding presence settled in the depths.

Suddenly, they broke through a barrier into a massive underwater cavern. The walls were lined with shimmering crystals, reflecting the pulsing light in a thousand directions. At the center of the cavern stood Kaldros, his figure imposing and menacing. He appeared as a dark silhouette against the radiant backdrop, his eyes glowing with malevolence.

"Ah, Jack and Lyria," Kaldros sneered, his voice echoing through the chamber. "How brave of you to return to my domain."

Jack stepped forward, his sword drawn, ready to face the sorcerer. "We're here to stop you, Kaldros. You won't take the Heart of Nalos."

Kaldros laughed, a chilling sound that sent shivers down Jack's spine. "You think you can defeat me? You're still naive, boy. This time, you're too late."

Before Jack could react, Kaldros raised his hand, summoning dark tendrils of energy that lashed out toward them. Lyria quickly conjured a shield of water, the magic swirling around them, blocking the dark energy.

"Stay close!" Lyria shouted, her voice strained as she focused on maintaining the barrier. Jack nodded, his heart racing as he kept his gaze fixed on Kaldros.

With a roar, Kaldros unleashed a wave of energy that shattered Lyria's shield, sending Jack and Lyria sprawling backward. The darkness enveloped them, and Jack felt a surge of panic. He glanced at Lyria, who was struggling to regain her footing.

"Lyria, we have to fight back!" Jack urged, pushing himself to his feet.

"Together," she replied, determination shining in her eyes. "We can do this."

Jack charged forward, his sword clashing against Kaldros's dark magic. The force of their struggle sent ripples through the water, and Jack could feel the power of their bond surging between them, giving him strength.

As they fought, Kaldros summoned tendrils of darkness that snaked toward them, but Jack and Lyria worked in tandem, dodging and countering his attacks. Lyria's magic lit the water with a dazzling glow, while Jack's sword sliced through the shadows, illuminating their path forward.

But Kaldros was relentless. He fought with an intensity that matched their own, and Jack could feel the weight of his power pressing down on them. With each blow, the tension in the water escalated, and Jack's resolve began to waver.

Facing the Darkness

"We can't let him overwhelm us!" Lyria shouted, her voice cutting through the chaos.

Jack nodded, summoning every ounce of strength within him. "We have to find a way to outsmart him. He thrives in darkness; we need to turn the tide."

With renewed determination, Jack focused on Lyria, channeling his energy into her magic. They began to weave their powers together, creating a dazzling vortex of light that pushed back against Kaldros's darkness.

Kaldros snarled, his expression twisted with rage. "You think your little tricks can defeat me? You are nothing!"

But Jack could see a flicker of uncertainty in Kaldros's eyes. They were gaining ground. "Lyria, now!" he called out.

With a fierce cry, Lyria unleashed a wave of radiant magic, directing it straight at Kaldros. The burst of light illuminated the cavern, pushing back against the shadows and forcing Kaldros to shield his eyes.

In that moment of vulnerability, Jack seized the opportunity. He charged forward, his sword raised high, ready to strike. As he swung, the blade caught the light of Lyria's magic, transforming it into a blinding beam that sliced through Kaldros's defenses.

"No!" Kaldros bellowed, the darkness around him dissipating as Jack's sword struck true. The sorcerer staggered backward, his power unraveling before their eyes.

But just as victory seemed within reach, Kaldros laughed, a haunting sound that echoed through the chamber. "You may have wounded me, but you will never defeat me! The Heart of Nalos is mine, and you are too late to stop it!"

Jack's heart sank as Kaldros vanished into a swirl of shadows, leaving only a lingering darkness behind. "We need to find him!" he shouted, but Lyria grabbed his arm, her expression grave.

"No, Jack. We need to focus on finding the Heart. He's using it to amplify his power, and we can't let him succeed."

Jack nodded, frustration boiling within him. They had come so close to defeating Kaldros, yet he had slipped through their fingers yet again.

The Search for the Heart

With Kaldros gone, Jack and Lyria turned their attention to the cavern, searching for any clues that might lead them to the Heart of Nalos. The crystal walls pulsed with energy, and Jack could feel a faint tug pulling him deeper into the cavern.

"This way!" he called, leading Lyria toward a series of tunnels that branched off from the main chamber. As they swam, the water shifted colors around them, swirling in shades of blue and green.

"What if Kaldros tries to stop us again?" Lyria asked, her voice steady but filled with concern.

"We'll be ready for him," Jack replied, determination etched on his face. "We've faced him before. We can do it again."

As they navigated the tunnels, the atmosphere grew tense. The once vibrant colors of the Abyssal Realm turned darker, the water thick with shadows. Jack felt a chill run down his spine as they pressed on, their hearts pounding in sync.

Eventually, they emerged into a vast chamber, the walls lined with shimmering stones that reflected the dim light. At the center of the room lay a pedestal, and atop it rested the Heart of Nalos—a radiant gem pulsing with an otherworldly glow.

A Heart of Light

Jack's breath caught in his throat as he approached the pedestal. The Heart of Nalos was even more magnificent than he had remembered, its colors swirling like a storm contained within the gem. It seemed to resonate with his very being, calling to him.

"Jack, be careful," Lyria cautioned, her eyes wide with awe. "Kaldros will likely have traps set around it."

"I know," Jack replied, his pulse quickening. He could feel the weight of destiny pressing down on him as he reached for the Heart.

Suddenly, a dark shadow flickered in the corner of his vision. Jack spun around just in time to see Kaldros emerging from the shadows, his form materializing like smoke in the water.

"You thought you could claim the Heart without consequence?" Kaldros hissed, his voice laced with malice. "Fools!"

Lyria quickly conjured a barrier of light, but Kaldros lashed out with a wave of darkness that shattered the barrier like glass. Jack felt the rush of energy as the darkness surged toward them, and he knew they had to act fast.

"We have to protect the Heart!" Jack shouted, positioning himself between Kaldros and the gem.

"Stay close!" Lyria urged, her voice steady as she prepared to summon her magic.

An Epic Showdown

As Kaldros advanced, Jack steeled himself for the confrontation. With Lyria beside him, they began to channel their combined powers, creating a shield of light that flickered against the encroaching darkness.

"Together!" Jack yelled, feeling the magic surge through them. The water around them shimmered with energy, and he could feel the weight of their bond amplifying their strength.

Kaldros snarled, rage boiling within him as he unleashed another wave of darkness. The collision of energies sent shockwaves through the chamber, and Jack felt the intensity of their battle reaching its peak.

With each blow, Jack and Lyria pushed back against Kaldros, their magic intertwining like vines in a storm. The light and darkness clashed violently, illuminating the cavern with a brilliant glow.

"Jack, now!" Lyria cried, her voice ringing with urgency. Jack launched forward, his sword aimed directly at Kaldros.

In that moment, everything slowed. Jack's heart raced as he swung his sword, and the blade connected with the dark energy surrounding Kaldros. The force of the impact sent ripples through the water, and Kaldros staggered back, momentarily stunned.

"Foolish children!" Kaldros roared, rage erupting from his lips. "You think you can defeat me?"

"Together!" Jack shouted again, focusing all his energy on the Heart of Nalos. The gem pulsed with light, responding to his call as if it recognized him as its rightful protector.

In a final surge of power, Jack and Lyria unleashed a wave of radiant magic, flooding the chamber with light. The darkness began to recede, Kaldros's form dissipating under the overwhelming energy.

"No!" Kaldros screamed, his figure vanishing into the shadows as he was consumed by the light.

With Kaldros defeated, Jack and Lyria stood amidst the brilliance of the Heart of Nalos, their hearts racing with triumph. They had faced their fears and emerged victorious.

Moving Forward

As they caught their breath, Jack turned to Lyria, a sense of relief flooding over him. "We did it."

"Yes, we did," Lyria replied, her eyes sparkling with pride. "But we can't let our guard down. Kaldros will return, and we need to be ready."

Jack nodded, determination etched on his face. They had proven their strength, but the true test lay ahead. The Heart of Nalos pulsed with energy in front of them, a beacon of hope guiding them on their journey.

As they prepared to claim the Heart, Jack felt a sense of purpose igniting within him. Together, they would uncover its secrets and protect it from those who sought to wield its power for darkness.

Jack and Lyria would face whatever challenges lay ahead—side by side, united in their quest for the Heart of Nalos. But first, they must return to the Oracle for further direction for the Heart of Nalos's safekeeping.

Chapter 13: The Weight of Choices

Returning to the Oracle

The journey back to the Oracle was filled with a mix of excitement and trepidation. Jack and Lyria swam through the vibrant waters of the Abyssal Realm, their hearts racing as they reflected on the recent battle with Kaldros. The Heart of Nalos pulsed gently in Jack's grip, its light providing a comforting glow amidst the darkness that had enveloped their fight.

"Do you think the Oracle will have the answers we seek?" Jack asked, glancing at Lyria as they swam side by side.

"I hope so," Lyria replied, her voice tinged with a mixture of hope and concern. "The Heart is powerful, but we need to know how to protect it. And what Kaldros's next move will be."

As they swam deeper, Jack couldn't help but admire the enchanting world around them. Bioluminescent creatures danced in the currents, casting an ethereal glow that illuminated their path. Every flicker of light reminded him of the stakes at hand; they were not just fighting for themselves, but for the future of Nalos.

After navigating a series of twisting tunnels, they finally reached the Oracle's new chamber—a vast cavern where light and shadow intertwined, creating a mesmerizing spectacle. The Oracle awaited them, seated on a throne made of iridescent coral, his eyes gleaming with ancient wisdom.

"Welcome back, brave souls," the Oracle intoned, his voice echoing through the chamber. "You have returned with the Heart of Nalos. A remarkable feat indeed."

Jack stepped forward, holding the Heart aloft. "We need your guidance. We must know how to protect it from Kaldros and where to take it for safekeeping."

The Oracle's gaze fell on the Heart, and a flicker of recognition sparked in his eyes. "The Heart is more than a mere gem; it is a vessel of great power. To ensure its safety, it must be placed in the *Place of Safekeeping*, a sanctuary beyond your current understanding."

"Really," He corrected himself, "to truly end Kaldros's threat, you need to banish him to the *Place of Lost Souls*, and to do that, you'll need a special kind of power."

Lyria felt a rush of urgency. "That sounds like a daunting task. First, I think we should just get the Heart to safety - how do we get there? What must we do?"

The Oracle raised his hand, summoning a swirling orb of light that floated between them. "This is the *Orb of Passage*. It can take you to the Place of Safekeeping, where the Heart of Nalos must reside."

Jack marveled at the orb's luminescence. "And it will keep the Heart safe?"

"Yes," the Oracle confirmed, his expression somber. "But there is more. Lyria, the orb holds a deeper purpose for you. It can also take you to the location where your parents have been held captive."

Lyria's heart raced, a mix of hope and despair flooding her veins. "My parents... I can finally find them?"

The Oracle nodded. "You stand at a crossroads, Lyria. The orb offers you two paths: one leads to the safety of the Heart, the other to the liberation of your parents. But you may only choose one."

Jack felt a pang of anxiety in his chest. "Lyria, whatever you choose, I'll support you."

Lyria stared at the orb, the weight of the decision bearing down on her. "I've been searching for my parents for so long. This might be my only chance..."

"But the Heart is crucial for the safety of Nalos" Jack urged gently. "Kaldros won't stop. We have to protect it."

Tears welled in Lyria's eyes as she grappled with the choice. "I don't know what to do. I want to save my parents, but I can't abandon the Heart. Nalos depends on it."

Making the Choice

The room felt heavy with silence as the Oracle observed the turmoil within Lyria. "Remember, dear one, this decision will shape your destiny. What weighs more heavily on your heart—the safety of Nalos, or the search for your family?"

Jack stepped closer, placing a reassuring hand on Lyria's shoulder. "We'll find a way to get to your parents after we secure the Heart. I promise you."

Lyria took a deep breath, steeling herself against the tempest of emotions. "You're right, Jack. The Heart must come first. We can't let Kaldros win. I choose to take the Heart to the Place of Safekeeping."

As she spoke the words, Jack could see the determination returning to her eyes, though they glistened with unshed tears. The Oracle nodded approvingly, the orb glowing brighter as Lyria made her choice.

"Very well," the Oracle said, his voice soothing. "Prepare yourselves for the journey ahead. The Orb of Passage will guide you to the Place of Safekeeping, but remain vigilant. Kaldros will not rest."

With a wave of his hand, the Oracle beckoned the orb closer. It hovered before them, radiating warmth and energy. "Focus on your destination—the Place of Safekeeping—and let the orb carry you."

Jack took Lyria's hand, and together they reached out, their fingers brushing against the orb's surface. The moment they made contact, a rush of energy surged through them, and the world around them began to dissolve into a whirlwind of light.

The Journey to the Place of Safekeeping

When the blinding light subsided, Jack and Lyria found themselves standing on a rocky outcrop overlooking a breathtaking landscape. The Place of Safekeeping sprawled before them, a mystical sanctuary nestled between towering mountains and crystalline lakes.

"Wow," Jack breathed, taking in the beauty of their surroundings. "This place is incredible."

Lyria nodded, her eyes wide with wonder. "It feels... safe. Like a refuge."

As they descended the rocky path, the vibrant colors of the landscape enveloped them—fields of luminescent flowers swayed gently in the breeze, and the air was filled with the sweet scent of nectar. It was a stark contrast to the darkness they had just escaped.

"Where exactly is the Heart supposed to go?" Jack asked, scanning the area for any signs of the sanctuary.

"The Oracle said it would be housed within a temple at the center of the Place of Safekeeping," Lyria explained. "We just need to find it."

As they ventured deeper into the sanctuary, the landscape gradually shifted. Ancient trees with twisting trunks formed a natural archway, leading them toward a grand structure that appeared to rise from the ground itself. The temple was adorned with intricate carvings and glowing crystals, radiating a soft light that beckoned them closer.

The Temple of the Heart

As they approached the temple, Jack felt a sense of reverence wash over him. "This must be it," he whispered, awed by the temple's beauty.

"Yes," Lyria replied, her voice barely above a whisper. "This is where the Heart of Nalos belongs."

With determination, they entered the temple, stepping into a vast chamber illuminated by the radiant light of the Heart. At the center of the room stood a pedestal, crafted from shimmering stone, ready to receive the Heart.

Jack's heart raced as he approached the pedestal, the Heart of Nalos still cradled in his hands. "This is it," he said, glancing back at Lyria. "Are you ready?"

"More than ever," she replied, her eyes reflecting the determination that had guided her choice.

Jack placed the Heart gently onto the pedestal. The moment it made contact, the entire chamber erupted with light, a surge of energy radiating outwards. The carvings on the walls glowed brightly, and a soft hum filled the air, as if the temple itself was rejoicing.

As the Heart settled into its new home, Jack felt a profound sense of relief wash over him. They had done it; the Heart was safe.

A Moment of Reflection

As the light began to fade, Lyria turned to Jack, her expression a mix of joy and sorrow. "We did it, Jack. The Heart is safe."

"Yes, but…" Jack hesitated, his heart heavy with the weight of Lyria's earlier choice. "You sacrificed the chance to find your parents for this."

"I did," Lyria said softly. "But it was the right choice. The Heart is vital for Nalos. We can still find them later, together."

Jack nodded, grateful for Lyria's strength. "We will find them, I promise. You're not alone in this."

Lyria smiled, though her eyes glistened with unshed tears. "Thank you, Jack. Your support means the world to me."

"Always," he replied, feeling the bond between them deepen. "We'll face whatever comes next, together."

Just then, the temple began to tremble, the walls shaking as if responding to an unseen force. Jack and Lyria exchanged worried glances, sensing that Kaldros's presence was still looming.

"We need to be ready," Jack said, his instincts kicking in. "Kaldros won't give up so easily."

Lyria's expression hardened with resolve. "We'll fight him if we have to. We won't let him take the Heart or hurt anyone else."

The Calm Before the Storm

As they stood together in the temple, the calm before the storm settled over them. The air was thick with tension, but Jack felt a renewed sense of purpose. They had safeguarded the Heart of Nalos, but their journey wasn't finished.

"Let's take a moment to gather our strength," Lyria suggested, her voice steady. "We'll need it for whatever comes next."

Jack nodded, closing his eyes for a moment to center himself. The warmth of the temple enveloped him, and he felt the Heart's energy pulsing nearby—a reminder of what they had achieved and what lay ahead.

As they caught their breath, Lyria took Jack's hand, her fingers intertwining with his. "Whatever happens, I'm glad we're in this together."

"Me too," Jack said, looking into her eyes. In that moment, the world around them faded, and all that mattered was the bond they shared.

As the tremors of the temple intensified, Jack knew that their next challenge was imminent. Kaldros would not rest, and the fight for the Heart of Nalos—and for Lyria's family—was only beginning.

Chapter 14: Shadows of the Past

The Aftermath of Safety

With the Heart of Nalos safely housed in the Place of Safekeeping, a sense of calm washed over Jack and Lyria. The overwhelming glow of the Heart radiated throughout the temple, casting gentle light upon their faces and illuminating the path forward. The immediate threat from Kaldros had been temporarily quelled, yet the shadows of his ambition lingered like a storm cloud on the horizon.

"We did it, Lyria," Jack said, turning to face her. "Nalos is safe for now."

"Yes, but we can't let our guard down," Lyria replied, her brow furrowed with concern. "Kaldros will stop at nothing to regain control of the Heart."

Jack felt the weight of their newfound responsibility pressing upon them. "We need to find a way to banish Kaldros to the Place of Lost Souls. But how do we even begin?"

Lyria bit her lip, contemplating their next steps. "To do that, we need allies and knowledge—someone who understands Kaldros's weaknesses and can guide us."

As they stood in the temple, a flicker of hope ignited within Jack. "What if we search for your parents first? They might have information about Kaldros or the magic he wields."

Lyria's eyes widened, her heart fluttering at the thought of reuniting with her family. "Yes! But we can't just wander aimlessly. We need someone who can help us find the right path."

Jack nodded, recalling the presence that had first brought him to this mystical realm. "We need to find the Deep One. He's the only one who can guide us and help us get started on our journey to rescue your parents."

The Call to the Deep One

With their minds set, Jack and Lyria prepared to leave the temple. The Orb of Passage glowed softly, willing to guide them to the next phase of their journey. As they clasped hands, Jack could feel Lyria's energy vibrating with excitement and determination.

"Let's go," Jack said, squeezing her hand gently.

They focused their thoughts on the Deep One, and the orb responded, swirling with light before engulfing them in its warmth.

When the luminescence faded, they found themselves standing at the edge of a vast, tranquil ocean. The waves lapped gently against the shore, and the sun dipped low on the horizon, casting golden rays over the water.

"Where are we?" Jack asked, taking in the stunning view.

"This is the entrance to the Abyssal Realm," Lyria replied, her eyes sparkling. "It's also where the Deep One resides, but we need to dive deep to find him."

"Let's not waste any time," Jack urged, his heart racing at the thought of confronting the ancient being.

Together, they stepped toward the water, the coolness enveloping them as they submerged. Lyria transformed into her mermaid form, her shimmering tail gliding gracefully through the water. Jack felt an overwhelming rush of air fill his lungs, a reminder of Lyria's magic allowing him to breathe underwater.

"Remember, you can breathe only because I'm here with you," Lyria said, glancing back at him with a smile. "If you were alone, you'd be lost."

"I won't forget that," Jack replied, admiration swelling in his chest. "Let's find the Deep One."

Into the Depths

As they swam deeper into the ocean, the world above faded into a serene silence, replaced by the rhythmic pulse of the waves. Strange, bioluminescent creatures flitted by, illuminating their path with dazzling colors. The further they descended, the darker and more mysterious their surroundings became.

"Do you think we're getting close?" Jack asked, straining to see through the depths.

"Yes, I can feel his presence," Lyria replied, her voice steady as she led the way. "The Deep One is powerful, but he may test us before he helps us."

As they approached a colossal underwater cavern, a strange energy filled the water, making Jack's skin tingle. The entrance was framed by jagged rocks adorned with vibrant coral and shimmering pearls.

Lyria paused, glancing back at Jack. "This is it. Are you ready?"

"Ready as I'll ever be," Jack responded, steeling himself.

They swam inside, the cavern opening up into another grand hall that felt alive with energy. The walls shimmered with ancient runes, and the air thrummed with a deep resonance. Here, a massive figure began to emerge from the shadows—the Deep One.

His form was fluid and ethereal, a swirling mass of water and light. He towered above them, his eyes deep and wise, reflecting the vastness of the ocean.

"Who dares to seek me in my domain?" the Deep One's voice resonated, echoing through the cavern.

"We seek your guidance, Great One," Lyria said, stepping forward, her heart pounding. "We need to find my parents and defeat Kaldros."

The Deep One regarded them with an intensity that made Jack's heart race. "Many have come seeking my help, but few understand the cost of my knowledge. What will you offer in exchange for my guidance?"

Jack exchanged a worried glance with Lyria, knowing they had little to offer. "We don't have much," he admitted. "But we're willing to risk everything to protect those we love."

The Deep One studied them for a long moment, the water around him swirling with energy. "Love is a powerful force, but it alone cannot guide you. You must prove your resolve. Face the trials of the Abyss, and only then shall I grant you the knowledge you seek."

The Trials of the Abyss

With that, the Deep One waved his hand, and the cavern transformed. The walls shifted, revealing three distinct paths illuminated by glowing orbs.

"Choose your path wisely," he instructed. "Each will test your strength, courage, and heart. Only by overcoming these trials can you earn my favor."

Jack felt a mix of fear and determination. "We're ready for whatever it takes."

Lyria nodded, her gaze fixed on the paths. "Let's face the trials together."

The First Trial

They stepped forward, choosing the left path. As they entered, the atmosphere shifted dramatically. The water grew colder, and shadows danced along the walls, whispering menacingly.

"Welcome, intruders," a shadowy figure hissed, emerging from the darkness. "You think you can pass our test?"

Jack clenched his fists, feeling the weight of the darkness surrounding them. "We're not afraid!"

The figure smirked, dark tendrils coiling around them. "Then face your fears!"

Suddenly, visions flooded Jack's mind—moments of doubt and insecurity. He saw his past failures, the times he had felt powerless, the fear of losing Lyria.

"Jack, don't listen!" Lyria urged, her voice breaking through the haze. "You're stronger than this!"

Summoning his inner strength, Jack pushed back against the shadows. "You don't control me! I won't be defined by my fears!"

With a fierce determination, he focused on the love he felt for Lyria and the bond they shared. The shadows recoiled, and the figure dissipated into nothingness, leaving only a shimmering orb behind.

"Your first trial is complete," the Deep One's voice echoed through the cavern. "You have proven your courage."

The Second Trial

Feeling invigorated, Jack and Lyria pressed on, choosing the middle path. This time, they found themselves surrounded by swirling currents, their bodies pulled in different directions.

"You must work together to find balance," the Deep One's voice resonated. "Only through unity can you navigate this trial."

"I can't hold on!" Jack shouted as the currents threatened to sweep him away.

"Focus on our bond!" Lyria called, reaching out to him. "We can do this!"

As they fought against the currents, Jack closed his eyes and pictured their connection—every adventure, every moment of laughter, and every shared fear. They were stronger together.

"Together!" they shouted in unison, their voices harmonizing.

With that, they linked hands, grounding each other. The currents began to calm, and the path ahead became clear. They moved forward, the water around them flowing gracefully as they emerged from the trial.

"Your second trial is complete," the Deep One proclaimed. "You have proven your unity."

The Final Trial

With their confidence soaring, they approached the last path. As they stepped into the chamber, the atmosphere thickened with anticipation. The Deep One's voice echoed once more.

"For your final trial, you must confront the darkness within your hearts. Only by embracing your true selves can you succeed."

The room darkened, and shadows began to form into twisted versions of Jack and Lyria, representing their deepest insecurities.

"You will never succeed," the shadowy Jack sneered. "You're not strong enough to defeat Kaldros. You'll fail."

"You don't belong here," the shadowy Lyria taunted. "You'll never find your parents. You're just a burden."

"No!" Lyria shouted, her voice steady. "I am strong! I am worthy of love and happiness!"

Jack took a deep breath, feeling the weight of doubt lift. "And I am not defined by my past! I will protect Lyria and find her parents!"

With renewed resolve, they faced their shadows. The darkness around them twisted, but their love shone brighter.

They reached out, their hands clasping the shadows, and in a moment of fierce determination, they pulled them into the light.

As the shadows dissolved, Jack and Lyria felt a wave of relief wash over them. The room brightened, revealing the Deep One once more.

"You have completed the trials," he declared, his voice filled with approval. "You have shown courage, unity, and truth. I will grant you the knowledge you seek."

Guidance from the Deep One

As the Deep One's form solidified, he extended a shimmering orb towards them. "This will guide you to your parents. Trust in your bond, and it will lead you to the truth."

Lyria reached for the orb, her heart racing with excitement. "Thank you, Great One!"

"But know this," the Deep One continued, his gaze piercing. "Your journey will not end with their rescue. Kaldros is still a threat, and you must prepare for the trials ahead."

"We will," Jack vowed, determination fueling his resolve. "We'll find a way to banish him."

With a nod, the Deep One released the orb into Lyria's hands. "Then go. The path to your parents awaits."

As they turned to leave, the water shimmered around them, and they felt a surge of hope. With the Deep One's guidance and the strength of their bond, Jack and Lyria knew they could face whatever lay ahead.

Setting Out for the Future

As they emerged from the cavern, the ocean stretched out before them, the sun casting a radiant glow across the water. Jack and Lyria exchanged a glance, their hearts full of hope and determination.

"Let's find my parents," Lyria said, gripping the orb tightly. "We'll bring them home."

"Yes," Jack replied, a warm smile breaking across his face. "Together, we can overcome anything."

As they prepared to set sail toward the unknown, Jack felt a rush of exhilaration. With the bond they shared, they were ready to face the challenges ahead, the shadows of their past now behind them.

Chapter 15: The Journey to Reunion

The Call of the Unknown

With the orb securely in Lyria's grasp, she and Jack felt an exhilarating mix of hope and trepidation. The ocean stretched out before them, shimmering in the golden sunlight as the waves beckoned them toward the horizon. The journey ahead was uncertain, but their bond fueled their resolve.

"Where do we start?" Jack asked, looking out at the vast expanse of water.

Lyria closed her eyes, holding the orb tightly as she felt its energy pulsing in her hand. "I think it will guide us," she said, her voice steady. "We just need to trust it."

Taking a deep breath, Jack nodded. "Alright. Let's see where it takes us."

As they focused their intentions on finding Lyria's parents, the orb began to glow brightly, illuminating the space around them. With a gentle pulse, it emitted a beam of light, pointing toward a distant cluster of islands on the horizon.

"Look!" Lyria exclaimed, her eyes widening with excitement. "It's leading us there!"

Jack felt a surge of hope. "Then let's go!" He dove into the water, Lyria following closely behind, their bodies cutting through the waves as they made their way toward the glowing destination.

The Island of Whispers

After a swift swim, they emerged on the shore of a small island shrouded in mist. The air was thick with mystery, and an ethereal quiet enveloped them. Jack looked around, intrigued by the unique beauty of the island. Giant trees with luminous leaves towered above them, their branches swaying gently in the breeze.

"Where are we?" Jack wondered aloud, scanning the surroundings.

"This is the Island of Whispers," Lyria replied. "It's said to be a place where lost souls gather, seeking solace and answers."

Jack's heart raced at the thought. "Could your parents be here?"

"I don't know," Lyria said, her expression contemplative. "But we should be cautious. The island has a reputation for playing tricks on those who enter."

As they ventured further onto the island, they were met with peculiar sights: trees that twisted into impossible shapes, flowers that glowed in every color of the rainbow, and streams that flowed with water as clear as crystal.

"Look at that!" Jack exclaimed, pointing to a nearby stream where delicate fish danced gracefully in the water. "This place is incredible!"

"It is," Lyria agreed, though her mind remained focused on her parents. "But we must stay alert. The island might test us."

The Whispering Winds

As they moved deeper into the island, a soft wind picked up, carrying with it a chorus of whispers. The sounds twisted around them, echoing words they couldn't quite decipher.

"Can you hear that?" Jack asked, straining to listen. "It sounds like voices."

"Yes," Lyria said, her expression shifting to one of concern. "They're trying to distract us. We need to stay focused on our goal."

Suddenly, the whispers grew louder, forming a cacophony of voices that surrounded them. Jack felt a chill run down his spine as he strained to make sense of the words.

"Turn back... Lost souls... You'll never find them..."

"Don't listen!" Lyria shouted, shaking her head to clear her mind. "We're not lost! We're here to find my parents!"

With determination, they pressed onward, blocking out the whispers as best they could. The landscape around them began to shift; trees morphed into shadowy figures that loomed over them, their branches stretching like claws.

"Stay close to me," Jack urged, instinctively reaching for Lyria's hand. She grasped it tightly, drawing strength from his presence.

As they continued, a sudden gust of wind swept through the clearing, and the shadows momentarily parted, revealing a hidden path.

The Guide in the Mist

"Look!" Lyria pointed ahead, where a figure emerged from the mist. It was an old man, draped in flowing robes that shimmered like the stars. His eyes sparkled with ancient wisdom, and he bore an otherworldly presence.

"I am Aelion, the guide of the Island of Whispers," he announced, his voice deep and melodic. "I have seen your journey and the bonds that bind you."

"Please, we're looking for my parents," Lyria pleaded. "Can you help us?"

Aelion regarded them thoughtfully. "The island holds many secrets, and its whispers can lead you astray. To find your parents, you must pass through the Trials of Clarity. Only then will the island reveal its truth."

Jack felt a wave of uncertainty wash over him. "What are the Trials of Clarity?"

"Three challenges that will test your heart, your mind, and your spirit," Aelion explained. "You must face your fears, uncover hidden truths, and demonstrate unwavering resolve."

"Will you help us?" Lyria asked, hope igniting in her eyes.

Aelion nodded. "I will be your guide, but you must summon the courage to face these trials. Trust in your bond, for it will light the way."

Trial One: The Illusion of Fear

They followed Aelion to a clearing surrounded by towering stones engraved with ancient symbols. The air felt heavy with anticipation as the old man gestured for them to step forward.

"The first trial is the Illusion of Fear," he explained. "You will face the fears that haunt your hearts. Only by confronting them can you overcome this challenge."

As he spoke, the stones began to glow, casting eerie shadows around them. Jack felt a knot of apprehension tighten in his stomach.

"What if I can't do it?" he muttered.

"You can," Lyria reassured him, squeezing his hand. "We'll face this together."

Suddenly, the atmosphere shifted, and the world around them warped. Jack found himself standing in a dark room, the air thick with despair. He turned to see a figure in the shadows—his past self, feeling lost and alone after losing his parents.

"Jack," the shadow said, its voice dripping with sorrow. "You'll always be alone. No one will ever care for you."

Jack's heart raced as memories flooded his mind—moments of abandonment and sorrow. He shook his head, trying to fight back the fear.

"No!" he shouted, grounding himself in the present. "I'm not alone anymore! I have Lyria!"

As he said her name, the shadows around him began to dissipate. Lyria's presence filled the space, radiating warmth and light.

"Jack, I'm here!" she called, her voice breaking through the darkness.

With a surge of determination, Jack reached for her. Their hands clasped together, and the darkness melted away, revealing the clearing once more.

"You have faced your fear," Aelion declared, nodding approvingly. "Now, onto the next trial."

Trial Two: The Truth Within

As they moved to the next clearing, Jack and Lyria felt a sense of anticipation mixed with dread. Aelion spoke again, his voice steady. "The second trial is the Truth Within. You must confront the truths you've hidden from yourselves."

The air shimmered, and a series of reflections appeared before them—images of their pasts flickered like old film reels. Jack watched as moments of doubt and shame played out: the sorrow of losing his family, the guilt of feeling abandoned, and the fear of being unworthy of love.

"Why can't I escape this?" he whispered, feeling the weight of the memories·pressing down on him.

"Jack, it's okay to feel these things," Lyria said softly, stepping closer. "But you have to acknowledge them to move forward."

With her support, Jack focused on the truth he had been avoiding. "I've felt unworthy of love because of my past," he admitted, his voice trembling. "I thought I was meant to be alone."

"No one is meant to be alone," Lyria replied, her eyes filled with understanding. "You have fought to find me, to be with me. That proves your strength."

Jack felt a wave of clarity wash over him as the reflections began to fade. "I'm not defined by my past. I can choose my future."

As he spoke those words, the reflections shattered like glass, revealing the sunlight pouring into the clearing once more.

"Your truth has set you free," Aelion proclaimed. "Now, prepare for the final trial."

Trial Three: The Resolve of Heart

With their spirits lifted, Jack and Lyria faced the last challenge. Aelion led them to a cliff's edge overlooking a vast ocean, the waves crashing violently against the rocks below.

"The final trial is the Resolve of Heart," he explained. "You must choose what you are willing to sacrifice for the ones you love."

Jack looked down at the turbulent waters, his heart pounding. "What do we have to sacrifice?"

"Only you can decide," Aelion replied, his gaze piercing. "Will you risk everything for your loved ones?"

As Jack stood at the edge, he thought about Lyria's parents—how much they meant to her and how desperately she wanted to reunite with them. He looked over at her, seeing the determination in her eyes, and felt a surge of love.

"I would sacrifice anything for you," he said, his voice strong. "You deserve to be with your family."

Tears filled Lyria's eyes as she squeezed his hand. "And I would do the same for you, Jack. We can't lose each other."

Suddenly, the ground beneath them began to shake, and the winds howled around them. Aelion raised his arms, urging them to stand firm.

"Speak your resolve!" he commanded. "Let the island know your intentions!"

"I will risk everything for Lyria's family!" Jack shouted, his heart racing. "I refuse to let fear dictate our fate!"

"I choose love over fear!" Lyria declared, her voice ringing with conviction. "I will do whatever it takes to bring my family home!"

As they spoke, the ground trembled violently, and a surge of energy surged through them. The waves below calmed, and the storm dissipated, revealing a tranquil sea once more.

"You have shown true resolve," Aelion announced, a proud smile on his face. "Your hearts are united in purpose. The island will guide you to your parents."

A New Path Forward

As the trials concluded, the island shimmered with newfound light. Aelion gestured for them to follow him back to the center of the island.

"The path to your parents is now open," he explained. "But remember, Kaldros is still a threat. You must be prepared for what lies ahead."

"We will be ready," Jack assured him, his heart filled with determination. "We've faced our fears and found strength in each other."

With a wave of his hand, Aelion summoned a map made of glimmering energy. It hovered before them, revealing the route to Lyria's parents.

"This will guide you to your parents," Aelion said. "Use it wisely."

"Thank you, Aelion," Lyria said, her heart swelling with gratitude. "We will find them."

As they took the map and turned to leave, Jack felt a renewed sense of purpose. With Lyria by his side, he knew they could face any challenge.

Chapter 16: The Reunion and the Hunt for Kaldros

The Journey to Her Parents Begins

The sun rose over the horizon, casting an ethereal glow over the ocean, as Jack and Lyria stood on the beach of the mystical island. The island shimmered with strange, luminous trees and creatures, their journey to this moment fraught with trials, dangers, and revelations. In Lyria's hand, the glowing map left behind by Aelion pulsed with energy, guiding them toward the next phase of their mission: finding Lyria's parents.

Jack glanced at Lyria, whose face was a mixture of anticipation and hope. For years, she had believed her parents to be lost forever, taken by unknown forces in this strange, otherworldly realm. But now, they were close, and the weight of the moment hung in the air.

"We'll find them, Lyria," Jack said, taking her hand. "We've come this far. Nothing will stop us now."

Lyria nodded, squeezing his hand tightly. "I know, Jack. And when we do... when we bring them back to Nalos, we'll be able to face Kaldros. Together."

With renewed determination, they set off, diving into the shimmering waters, as Lyria transformed once more into her mermaid form. Her long, flowing tail glistened beneath the surface, guiding Jack effortlessly through the water. Though he still marveled at his ability to breathe underwater with her presence, the weight of their mission left no room for distraction. The journey ahead was dangerous, but together, they could overcome anything.

The Hidden Cavern of Lyria's Parents

The orb guided them toward an uncharted section of the ocean. As they descended into the depths, the light around them faded, and the water grew colder. Soon, the outline of a massive underwater cavern appeared before them, its entrance guarded by strange, glowing creatures.

"This is it," Lyria said, her voice tense with anticipation. "This is where they've been kept."

The cavern was eerily silent as they approached, the stillness only broken by the occasional flicker of bioluminescent light from the creatures that floated around the entrance. Jack felt a shiver run down his spine.

"Are you ready?" Jack asked, glancing at Lyria.

"I've been ready for this moment my entire life," she replied, her voice strong. "Let's go."

They swam into the cavern, and as they moved deeper inside, the walls began to glow with soft, green light, illuminating their path. After what felt like an eternity of navigating the maze-like tunnels, they finally entered a large, open chamber. At the far end of the room, two figures sat, their forms faintly glowing in the dim light.

"Mom… Dad…" Lyria's voice trembled as she moved forward, her heart racing.

The figures stirred, and as they turned to face her, the recognition in their eyes was instant. They were thinner, their faces marked with the weariness of captivity, but they were alive.

"Lyria?" her mother's voice cracked, disbelief and joy mingling in her tone. "Is it really you?"

"Yes!" Lyria cried, rushing forward, embracing her parents tightly. "I've found you. After all these years, I've found you."

Jack hung back, watching the emotional reunion unfold. It was a moment of pure joy, but he knew they couldn't stay here long. The threat of Kaldros was still looming, and they needed to get Lyria's parents to safety.

"We have to move," Jack said gently, stepping forward. "We'll explain everything later, but for now, we need to get you both back to Nalos. Kaldros is still hunting us, and we can't let him find you."

Lyria's parents nodded, tears in their eyes. They trusted their daughter, and now, they trusted Jack.

The Return to Nalos

The journey back to Nalos was swift and filled with a sense of urgency. Lyria's parents, weak from their long captivity, leaned on Jack and Lyria for support as they swam through the ocean. The island of Nalos shimmered in the distance, a beacon of safety amidst the chaos of the surrounding world.

As they reached the shore, Lyria transformed back into her human form, helping her parents onto the sandy beach. Jack followed closely, scanning the horizon for any sign of danger.

"They'll be safe here," Lyria said, her voice steady. "But we can't waste any more time. We need to stop Kaldros before he finds a way to gain control of the Heart of Nalos again."

Lyria's parents looked at her with concern. "You're not going after him, are you?" her father asked, his voice filled with worry.

"We have to," Lyria replied, her expression resolute. "Kaldros won't stop until he has control of the Heart. If we don't banish him to the Place of Lost Souls, he'll always be a threat to Nalos... and to all of us."

Her mother nodded, though fear flickered in her eyes. "Just promise us you'll be careful."

"I promise," Lyria said softly. "But we have to do this."

The Hunt for Kaldros Begins

With Lyria's parents safely in Nalos, Jack and Lyria began their preparations to confront Kaldros. The map from Aelion had revealed Kaldros' current stronghold—a dark fortress deep in the Abyssal Realm. It was a place of nightmares, filled with twisted creatures and treacherous waters.

"We have to be smart about this," Jack said as they gathered their supplies. "Kaldros is powerful, and we can't afford to make any mistakes."

Lyria nodded in agreement. "It's not just Kaldros we need to worry about—the entire realm is filled with dangers. We've barely scratched the surface on our previous visits."

Despite the risks, they knew this was their only chance. Kaldros had to be banished, or he would continue to hunt them, seeking control over the Heart of Nalos.

"Once we find him, how do we banish him?" Jack asked, thinking through their plan. "The Oracle said it required a special kind of power."

Lyria held up the glowing orb that had guided them on their journey. "This will help. The Oracle told me that the same magic that keeps the Heart of Nalos safe can also be used to send Kaldros to the Place of Lost Souls. But it won't be easy. He'll fight us with everything he has."

"Then we'll fight back," Jack said, determination in his voice. "We're not alone in this. We have each other."

Into the Abyssal Fortress

The journey back to the Abyssal Realm was fraught with tension. As they descended deeper into the ocean, the water around them grew darker and colder, the light from the surface fading into obscurity. Strange, eerie creatures swam around them, their eyes glowing in the darkness as they watched the intruders pass by.

"This place still gives me the creeps," Jack muttered, glancing around warily.

Lyria's eyes were sharp, her senses attuned to the dangers lurking in the depths. "We're getting close. I can feel his presence."

Ahead of them, a massive structure loomed in the distance. The Abyssal Fortress stood like a monolith, its jagged spires rising from the ocean floor. It was a place of shadows, where Kaldros had built his stronghold.

"There it is," Lyria said, her voice barely a whisper. "That's where he's hiding."

They approached cautiously, weaving through the maze of underwater tunnels that led to the fortress. Every step was measured, every sound amplified by the oppressive silence of the deep. Jack's heart pounded in his chest, but he kept his focus on the task ahead.

As they neared the entrance, two enormous, twisted creatures emerged from the shadows, their eyes glowing red with malice. Kaldros' sentinels.

"Get ready," Lyria said, gripping her trident tightly.

The creatures lunged toward them, their massive bodies cutting through the water with terrifying speed. Jack dodged the first attack, narrowly avoiding the creature's razor-sharp claws. Lyria countered with a powerful strike, her trident glowing with magical energy as it pierced through one of the creatures' armor.

The battle was fierce, but Jack and Lyria fought in perfect sync. Together, they overwhelmed the sentinels, defeating them one by one. As the last creature fell, the entrance to the fortress lay before them, unguarded.

Confronting Kaldros

Inside the fortress, the atmosphere was thick with darkness. Shadows clung to the walls, and the air was cold and oppressive. They moved quietly through the halls, their footsteps echoing in the silence.

At the heart of the fortress, they found him.

Kaldros stood before the throne of the Abyssal Realm, his eyes glowing with malevolent power. His dark, twisted form radiated evil, and a cruel smile spread across his face as he saw them enter.

"So, you've come," Kaldros hissed, his voice dripping with malice. "I was wondering when you would show yourselves."

"This ends here, Kaldros," Lyria said, her voice steady despite the fear she felt. "We're going to banish you to the Place of Lost Souls, where you belong."

Kaldros laughed, a low, menacing sound. "You think you can defeat me? You're nothing compared to my power."

Jack stepped forward, his sword at the ready. "We'll see about that."

The final confrontation was about to begin, and the fate of Nalos—and Lyria's family—hung in the balance.

Chapter 17: The Final Battle Against Kaldros

The Calm Before the Storm

The dim light of the Abyssal Fortress flickered ominously as Jack and Lyria faced Kaldros. The dark entity loomed before them, his twisted form filling the cavernous throne room with an aura of malevolence. Jack tightened his grip on his sword, while Lyria's trident shimmered with magical energy, the two weapons a reflection of their determination to end this once and for all.

The oppressive weight of the Abyssal Realm seemed to press in from all sides. The stillness in the room was unsettling, like the eerie calm before a storm. Jack could feel the tension in the air, the anticipation of what was to come building up inside him.

"This ends now, Kaldros," Jack said, his voice steady, though his heart pounded in his chest.

Kaldros sneered, his glowing red eyes locking onto them with unholy fury. "You think you can banish me? I am eternal! This realm is mine!"

"Not anymore," Lyria retorted, stepping forward beside Jack. "We're here to send you to the Place of Lost Souls, where you can never return. The power to do so is with us!"

The malevolent being let out a low growl, his form shifting and contorting as dark tendrils of energy began to snake around him. "You dare challenge me? You will regret this!"

And with that, the battle began.

The First Strike

Kaldros moved with terrifying speed, launching himself toward Jack and Lyria with a roar. Shadows erupted from his hands, slashing through the air like whips of darkness. Jack barely had time to react as he raised his sword to block the first strike, the force of the blow sending a shockwave through his arms.

Lyria was quick on her feet, diving to the side as Kaldros' tendrils lashed toward her. Her trident glowed as she called upon the power of the magic orb, channeling its energy into her weapon. With a sharp cry, she thrust her trident forward, sending a wave of light crashing into Kaldros.

The impact staggered him, but only for a moment. He roared in fury, his dark form flickering as he summoned more power from the Abyssal Realm. The ground beneath them trembled, and jagged spires of rock shot up from the floor, forcing Jack and Lyria to move quickly to avoid being impaled.

"He's drawing strength from this place!" Jack shouted as he narrowly avoided a spike of rock.

"I know!" Lyria responded, her voice strained. "We have to weaken him!"

Jack slashed at the dark tendrils, cutting through them with his sword, but for every one he severed, more took its place. Kaldros was relentless, his power seemingly endless as he lashed out at them from all directions.

But Jack and Lyria were not without their own strengths. Working in perfect harmony, they dodged and countered every attack, their movements fluid and in sync. Jack struck with precision, while Lyria used her magical abilities to shield them from Kaldros' darkest attacks.

Pushing Back the Darkness

As the battle raged on, the room seemed to darken even further, Kaldros drawing more of the Abyssal Realm's power to fuel his attacks. The shadows around him thickened, swirling like a storm as he unleashed a torrent of dark energy.

"Enough of this!" Kaldros bellowed, his voice echoing through the chamber. "You are nothing compared to me!"

A massive wave of energy erupted from him, sending both Jack and Lyria flying backward. Jack hit the ground hard, the impact knocking the wind from his lungs. His sword clattered to the floor beside him, and for a brief moment, the world spun around him.

Lyria was thrown against the wall, her body slamming into the stone with a sickening thud. She gritted her teeth, forcing herself to her feet despite the pain that shot through her limbs. Her vision swam, but she could still see Kaldros standing at the center of the room, his form towering and menacing.

"We can't let him win," Lyria murmured to herself, gripping her trident tightly. She glanced over at Jack, who was struggling to stand, his body bruised and battered.

"Jack!" she called out, rushing to his side.

"I'm okay," Jack groaned, grabbing his sword and pushing himself to his feet. "We need to find a way to stop him."

Lyria nodded, her mind racing. They had to weaken Kaldros' connection to the Abyssal Realm, to sever the power that was keeping him strong. But how?

As if sensing her thoughts, Kaldros let out a twisted laugh. "You cannot defeat me. The Abyssal Realm bends to my will. I am its master!"

But as Kaldros continued his tirade, Lyria's eyes caught a faint glimmer of light near the throne—an ancient symbol etched into the stone floor. The same symbol that had been used to seal the Heart of Nalos, a symbol of protection and banishment.

"That's it," Lyria whispered. "Jack! The symbol on the floor— if we can activate it, we can sever his connection to the Abyssal Realm!"

The Desperate Plan

Jack followed Lyria's gaze and saw the symbol. "It's our only chance," he said, nodding in agreement. "But how do we activate it?"

"We'll have to channel the power of the orb through it," Lyria explained. "But it's going to take everything we have."

Without hesitation, the two rushed toward the symbol, dodging Kaldros' attacks as he lashed out in fury. He could sense their plan and was determined to stop them. The room shook violently as more spikes of rock erupted from the floor, and shadows clawed at them with relentless aggression.

Lyria reached the symbol first, kneeling beside it as she pressed her hand to the stone. The orb, still glowing faintly around her neck, began to pulse with energy, responding to her touch. Jack stood beside her, his sword at the ready as he fended off Kaldros' attacks.

"Hurry!" Jack shouted as he blocked another dark tendril.

"I'm trying!" Lyria replied, her voice strained as she focused all her energy on activating the symbol.

The ground beneath them began to glow with a soft, golden light, the ancient magic of the island awakening as Lyria channeled the orb's power into the symbol. Slowly, the light spread outward, creating a barrier of energy that began to push back the shadows.

Kaldros screamed in rage as the light began to weaken his connection to the Abyssal Realm. His dark form flickered as the shadows around him dissipated.

The Final Stand

With a roar of fury, Kaldros made one final, desperate attack, launching himself toward Jack and Lyria with all the strength he had left. Dark energy crackled around him, his form contorting and twisting as he sought to destroy them before the light could fully banish him.

But Jack was ready.

As Kaldros lunged forward, Jack raised his sword, channeling the power of the orb through the blade. With a swift, powerful strike, he brought the sword down, cutting through Kaldros' form and severing his connection to the Abyssal Realm entirely.

Kaldros let out a deafening scream as his body began to disintegrate, the shadows that had once surrounded him evaporating into the air. The dark energy that had fueled him was gone, and with it, his power.

"No!" Kaldros howled as he began to fade, his form becoming more and more transparent. "You cannot do this! I am eternal!"

But it was too late. The orb with the power from the Heart of Nalos had done its work.

With one final, agonized cry, Kaldros was banished to the Place of Lost Souls, his form disappearing into the void. The air around them grew still, the oppressive darkness of the Abyssal Realm lifting as Kaldros was finally gone.

Victory at Last

Jack and Lyria stood in the center of the room, breathing heavily as the glow of the symbol faded. It was over. Kaldros was gone, banished to the Place of Lost Souls forever. There would be no return for him, no more threats to the Heart of Nalos or the island.

Lyria turned to Jack, her eyes filled with relief and exhaustion. "We did it," she whispered.

Jack nodded, pulling her into a tight embrace. "It's over," he said softly. "He's gone."

For the first time in what felt like an eternity, they allowed themselves a moment of peace. Nalos and the Heart were safe. And together, they had overcome the darkness.

With Kaldros defeated, there were still mysteries left to uncover—Lyria's parents, the Heart's true purpose, and the future of Nalos.

For now, though, they could rest, knowing that the greatest battle had been won.

Chapter 18: A New Beginning in Nalos

The Calm After the Storm

The air around Nalos was different now. The weight of Kaldros' dark influence had lifted, and for the first time in what felt like a lifetime, Jack and Lyria felt a sense of peace. The Heart of Nalos was safe, its brilliance restored, and the island itself seemed to be flourishing in the absence of the dark energy that had plagued it for so long.

Jack stood on a cliff overlooking the sparkling waters, the gentle breeze playing through his hair as he watched the waves lap peacefully against the shore. Lyria, standing beside him, looked equally serene, though Jack could sense that something was on her mind.

"They're free," Lyria whispered, her voice filled with relief. "The island, the Heart—everything is free from Kaldros."

Jack smiled, reaching for her hand. "And so are we."

But even as they basked in the aftermath of their victory, the reality of what came next was starting to settle in. They had saved Nalos, but there were still choices to be made, especially for Jack.

As the thought lingered, a deep, resonant voice echoed across the wind, shaking both of them from their moment of reflection.

"Jack. Lyria. Come to me."

The voice was unmistakable—the Deep One. It was a voice that carried weight, reverberating through the earth itself. Jack and Lyria exchanged a glance before turning and making their way toward the source of the summons.

Summoned by the Deep One

They moved quickly, traversing the now peaceful landscape, making their way back to the shores where the Deep One had first revealed himself to Jack. The waters were calm, but they held a kind of power, as though the very essence of the island was gathering around them.

When they arrived, the great figure of the Deep One emerged from the depths of the ocean, his form towering above them, ancient and wise. His eyes glowed softly, and his voice, when he spoke, seemed to hum through the air like a melody carried by the wind.

"I, and Nalos, are grateful for your efforts," the Deep One began, his voice calm and commanding. "You have proven yourselves to be very brave. For this, I will grant you a great gift, Jack—a one-way trip back to your former home, where all of this will soon become nothing more than a strange dream, soon to be forgotten."

Jack's heart stopped for a moment as the words sunk in. A one-way trip back home. To the life he had known before the island, before Lyria, before the Heart of Nalos. A chance to return to the world he once knew, where the only dangers were the mundane struggles of survival as a fisherman, not the mystical forces he had faced here.

He felt Lyria's eyes on him, and when he turned to look at her, he saw the uncertainty on her face. It was a choice—one that only he could make.

"My life back home..." Jack started, his voice steady but contemplative. "It was anything but life or home. I was an orphan, raised by an old fisherman. My parents died when I was young in a terrible wreck. After my guardian passed, there was nothing left for me. But here..." He paused, looking at Lyria, feeling the warmth of her presence beside him. "I've found new life here. With Lyria. And I would like to find a new home here, too."

The Deep One watched them for a moment, as though weighing the sincerity of Jack's words. His massive form shifted, the water rippling around him as he spoke again, his voice filled with quiet understanding. "You realize the gravity of what you ask? This is an eternal decision."

Jack nodded, unshaken. "I understand. My place is here. With her."

There was a long pause before the Deep One finally spoke again. "So be it. Your wish is granted."

The air seemed to shimmer around them as the Deep One's power settled over Jack, binding him to the land and the waters of Nalos. There would be no going back—not that Jack would ever want to. This was his home now.

The Deep One gave one final nod, his glowing eyes softening slightly as he looked between Jack and Lyria. "You have earned more than just my gratitude. I owe you both a debt that cannot be repaid. But perhaps you will accept this gift."

The great being gestured toward the vast horizon beyond Nalos, where dozens of islands dotted the shimmering sea. "You may choose any island you wish. It will be yours—a place to call home, where you may live in peace."

Reunited with Family

Before they could choose their new home, however, there was one final reunion that had to happen. Lyria's parents, lost for so long, awaited them back on the main island. The thought of seeing them again filled Lyria with a sense of urgency and excitement that had been missing during the long battle against Kaldros.

When they arrived, Jack watched as Lyria rushed ahead, her heart racing as she called out for her mother and father. They rushed to meet her right away.

Tears welled up in Lyria's eyes as she ran to them, pulling them both into an embrace. "Mother! Father! I missed you so much!"

Her mother smiled, tears in her own eyes as she stroked Lyria's hair. "We always knew you'd find us. We never lost hope."

Her father's voice was warm and filled with pride. "You've grown so much, Lyria. And you've saved us all."

Jack stood back, watching them with a smile. He could feel the love and joy radiating from Lyria's family, and it filled his heart with warmth. He knew that this was the moment Lyria had been waiting for, and he was honored to witness it.

After a few moments, Lyria turned to him, taking his hand. "Jack, this is my family. And now, you're part of it too."

Jack bowed his head slightly in respect. "It's an honor."

Her father stepped forward, placing a hand on Jack's shoulder. "You saved our daughter and helped bring peace to Nalos. You have our eternal gratitude."

A New Home Among the Islands

With Lyria's parents safely returned to Nalos, it was time for Jack and Lyria to make their decision—to choose the island where they would build their new home. The Deep One's gift was one of incredible generosity, and the options before them seemed limitless.

They sailed across the calm seas, passing by island after island, each one more beautiful than the last. Some were lush with vibrant jungles, others boasted towering mountains or golden beaches. But it wasn't until they reached an island at the farthest edge of the archipelago that they knew they had found the one.

It was a place unlike any they had seen before. The island was surrounded by a crystal-clear lagoon, its waters shimmering in shades of blue and green. White sandy beaches stretched for miles, leading into rolling hills covered in soft grass and wildflowers. At the heart of the island was a hidden cove, where a waterfall cascaded down from a cliff, filling the air with the soothing sound of rushing water.

"This is it," Lyria whispered, her voice filled with awe as they stood on the beach, gazing out at the horizon.

Jack nodded, his heart swelling with contentment. "It's perfect."

The island felt like a sanctuary—enchanted and serene, a place where they could build a life together, free from the chaos of their past. It was a place where they could finally rest, where they could create a future together, surrounded by the beauty and magic of Nalos.

As they stood there, hand in hand, the sun setting over the horizon, Jack knew that this was the beginning of something new. He had come to this realm by accident, but now, he couldn't imagine being anywhere else. Nalos was his home, and with Lyria by his side, his life was complete.

Chapter 19: A New Home, A New Beginning

The Island Sanctuary

Jack and Lyria stood on the white sand of their island, gazing at the waves gently kissing the shore. It was the island they had chosen. The gentle breeze whispered through the palm trees, and the sound of the waterfall cascading down the cliffs in the distance filled the air with a peaceful rhythm.

Behind them, Lyria's parents walked side by side, their hands clasped, their faces still filled with gratitude and awe for the place they would now call home. It had been a long journey, but now, at last, they could begin a new chapter of their lives, one filled with peace, wonder, and family.

"This is more than I ever could have hoped for," Lyria whispered as she pressed her head against Jack's shoulder. "It's perfect."

Jack squeezed her hand and looked out over the lagoon. "It's beautiful, Lyria. More than I could have ever imagined. It's not just an island; it feels like it's alive with magic."

And indeed, it was. The island seemed to hum with an energy, an aura of enchantment that promised not just peace but endless possibilities.

The Arrival of Mystical Helpers

One afternoon, as they explored more of the island, something extraordinary happened.

From the dense jungle came the sound of rustling, followed by the appearance of several small figures. They were unlike anything Jack or Lyria had ever seen before—absurdly mystical creatures with round, glowing eyes, shimmering skin that changed colors in the sunlight, and elongated fingers that moved with surprising grace. These beings were neither threatening nor alarming; instead, they radiated a friendly energy.

The leader of these beings, who stood no taller than Jack's waist, stepped forward and bowed with a deep flourish.

"We are the Sylphrians," the being said in a voice that was both deep and melodic. "Sent by the magic of Nalos to help you, as you have helped the land. Your bravery has granted you more than just an island—it has given you a new home. And we are here to build it."

Lyria's eyes widened in wonder. "Build our home?"

The Sylphrian leader smiled, his eyes glowing softly. "Yes. A house more beautiful than any dream. A place where you and your family will live in peace. We will begin at once."

Before Jack or Lyria could speak, the Sylphrians sprang into action. They moved with incredible speed, gathering materials from the jungle and the surrounding landscape. Large palm leaves, enchanted driftwood, and stones that shimmered with a strange light were transformed in their hands into building materials. With a mere flick of their glowing fingers, the Sylphrians began constructing what would become a grand mansion—a home more stunning than either Jack or Lyria could have ever imagined.

A Grand Mansion

By the next morning, the mansion was nearly complete. Jack and Lyria stood back in awe as they beheld the structure rising before them. It was a sprawling, elegant home with high, arching windows that reflected the surrounding beauty of the island. A wide wrap-around porch encircled the entire mansion, offering panoramic views of the beach, the lagoon, and the jungle.

The porch itself was lined with intricately carved wooden railings, each one imbued with Sylphrian magic, making the wood glow faintly in the moonlight. Hanging lanterns of glowing orbs drifted above the porch, casting soft light as they swayed gently in the breeze.

The mansion was grand yet intimate, filled with charm and magic. The interior was open and airy, with sweeping staircases leading to upper balconies, cozy nooks, and large windows that bathed each room in sunlight. Every inch of the house seemed alive with the magic of Nalos, from the enchanted fireplace that roared without fuel, to the walls that shimmered like the surface of the sea.

"It's...breathtaking," Lyria whispered, her voice full of awe.

"This is our home," Jack said, his heart full as he wrapped his arm around Lyria. "Our real home."

Outside the mansion, the land was equally enchanted. Magical fruit trees sprang up along the edges of the property, their branches heavy with brightly colored fruit that shimmered with an inner glow. The air around the trees was fragrant with the scent of exotic blossoms, and the fruit itself was sweeter than anything they had ever tasted.

The land was dotted with strange and wonderful landmarks: a small pond that sparkled in shades of pink and gold; stones that sang when the wind passed through them; flowers that bloomed in iridescent patterns, their petals changing color with the light of day. It was a paradise like no other.

Lyria's parents stood in silence, overcome by the sheer beauty of the place.

"I never imagined I'd live to see something like this," Lyria's mother said softly, her eyes wet with emotion.

"You deserve this," Jack said, his voice filled with warmth. "We all do."

A Mysterious Discovery

For weeks, Jack, Lyria, and her parents settled into their new life. Each day was filled with joy and peace as they explored the island, swam in the lagoon, and ate the magical fruit that seemed to rejuvenate their spirits.

One evening, as the sun began to dip below the horizon, casting a golden glow over the island, Jack and Lyria ventured deeper into the jungle. They had explored most of their new home, but the island was large, and there were still places left undiscovered.

As they walked hand in hand, the trees overhead grew thicker, their branches forming a natural canopy that shielded them from the fading sunlight. The air grew cooler, and a sense of mystery filled the atmosphere.

After a while, they stumbled upon a clearing, and in the center of it was something neither of them expected: a large, weathered trunk. It was old, covered in vines and moss, as though it had been forgotten there for centuries.

"What is this?" Lyria asked, stepping closer to the trunk.

Jack knelt down, examining the strange markings that adorned the sides of the trunk. They were symbols he had never seen before, etched deep into the wood as though by some ancient hand.

"Only one way to find out," Jack said as he reached for the latch.

It took a moment of effort, but with a creak, the trunk popped open. Inside, they found glittering treasures—coins made of pure gold, gemstones that shone with an otherworldly light, and intricately designed artifacts that seemed to hum with magic.

But among the treasure was something else. Tucked beneath a pile of gold coins was a scroll, sealed with wax and an unfamiliar insignia.

Jack carefully pulled it out and unrolled it.

"What does it say?" Lyria asked, peering over his shoulder.

The words were written in an ancient language, but somehow, they could both understand the message.

The Call to Adventure

"To those who find this treasure, know that it is but a fraction of what awaits you. If you are brave, if you are bold, venture forth and seek the Lost Realms. There, you will find riches beyond measure…and mysteries that may never be solved. The choice is yours. But be warned: once you begin the journey, there is no turning back."

Jack and Lyria exchanged glances, their hearts racing.

"The Lost Realms?" Lyria whispered, her eyes alight with curiosity.

Jack smiled, feeling the familiar thrill of adventure coursing through his veins. "Looks like we've just been invited on another adventure."

The sun had now set completely, and the clearing was bathed in the soft glow of moonlight. The island was peaceful, and their new home was waiting for them. But in that moment, both Jack and Lyria knew that their story was far from over.

They had found peace, they had found family, but now, standing before this mysterious trunk, they realized they still had the heart of adventurers. And somewhere, out there in the Lost Realms, a new journey awaited.

"We could stay here," Lyria said with a smile, "live out our days in peace."

Jack grinned, pulling her close. "We could. Or we could see what's out there."

Lyria laughed softly, leaning into him. "One more adventure?"

Jack kissed her gently on the forehead. "For tonight, let's just enjoy the moonlight."

The End?

www.ingramcontent.com/pod-product-compliance
Lightning Source LLC
Chambersburg PA
CBHW032031050726

47590CB00006B/2375